KU-015-288

The Scattergun Gang

The Scattergun Gang were the worst bunch of killers that Texas had ever seen and they had Josh McCall's wife as a hostage.

There were no definite clues, only a relentless trail through the Indian Territory, a place infested with outlaws on the run – all with an eye for a fast buck and all willing to put a bullet in your back if that was what it took.

But McCall was ready to take them all on, even if he had to use his bare hands. . . .

Nothing would stop him getting Rosa back. Nothing.

The Scattergun Gang

Hank J. Kirby

A Black Horse Western

ROBERT HALE · LONDON

© Hank J. Kirby 2011
First published in Great Britain 2011

ISBN 978-0-7090-9139-4

Robert Hale Limited
Clerkenwell House
Clerkenwell Green
London EC1R 0HT

www.halebooks.com

The right of Hank J. Kirby to be identified as
author of this work has been asserted by him
in accordance with the Copyright, Designs and
Patents Act 1988

MORAY COUNCIL LIBRARIES & INFO.SERVICES	
20 32 07 32	
Askews & Holts	
WF WF	

Typeset by
Derek Doyle & Associates, Shaw Heath
Printed and bound in Great Britain by
CPI Antony Rowe, Chippenham and Eastbourne

CHAPTER 1

RAW DEAL

The explosion was the biggest the town had heard since the Yankee siege back in '64. Then the town had been pummelled mercilessly for three days by rows of cannon that stretched along the entire crest of Misery Mountain. Most of the town had been reduced to rubble before the Yankee commander, Colonel Liam Borthwick, decided to recognize the tattered white and bloodstained shirt belonging to the Reb captain, whipping in the wind on top of a crooked sapling cut for the purpose. It had been there for two whole days.

But that had been sixteen years ago. . . . *This* explosion was in the Jacksboro Branch of the North Texas Cattlemen's Bank.

It had blown out the east wall, the hurtling red bricks demolishing most of the Land Agency across the alley, killing the agent outright. The chief male clerk had one leg so badly mauled it was later amputated. Miss Louise

Kitner, the auburn-haired *receptioniste*, had most of her voluminous skirts and undergarments blown off her exciting white body: there were far more volunteers than were needed, clearing away the rubble around her office: *far more*!

The Banker, Keir Redmond, was killed at his desk, in the midst of refusing a loan to the owner of one of the outlying ranches. The rancher would never need the loan now: he died of injuries a week later.

Two clerks died in their cages and three customers were seriously injured, half-a-dozen others less seriously.

That was the immediate toll, but there was more to come.

And it came in the shadowy shapes of seven, some said nine, bandanna-masked men blundering through the thick clouds of dust and powdersmoke into the wreckage of the bank interior. They stumbled through the huge ragged hole in what was left of the east wall, groped their way into what had once been kown as the Secure Room where the large safe was set, bolted and cemented to the floor. The extra-heavy door was blown off completely, and much of the safe interior wrecked. Canvas bags stencilled with the words Cattleman's Bank, Jacksboro, Texas, a couple smouldering from the heat of the explosion, had survived in their metal carry box, though the lid was missing, the hinges twisted like candy.

The masked men all held double-barrelled, sawn-off shotguns, the right barrel loaded with double-0 buckshot, the left with a handful of rocksalt.

The leader, Scattergun Kane, had a twisted sense of humour, claimed the salt was for anyone who felt a powerful, overwhelming urge to be heroic: the salt would stop such a man in his tracks, stinging like all get-out, occasionally ripping a flabby neck or cheek, once blinding a would-be hero. Most decided to just let things happen as they writhed about in pain . . . the buckshot, however, was for those who weren't deterred by the salt. It guaranteed the glory-hunter the possibility of posthumous recognition, even a fancy headstone in the local Boot Hill . . . seemed plumb loco to Kane, but long ago he had given up trying to figure out the way some folk thought they had to play the hero. *Damn idiots!*

He was just an average-sized man, now looked around the carnage and desctruction in the office, steel-grey eyes pinched-down above the bandanna. 'Where's that goddam Nitro?' he rasped, the powder-smoke penetrating the mask and hacking at his throat. 'Fool used enough dynamite to turn Misery Mountain into rubble!'

'I found him, easy,' spoke up a lean man in dusty, ragged clothes, obviously big-nosed, the way his mask hung over his features, the lower part standing inches out from his jaw. When Kane turned, the man gestured to a small section of wall that hadn't yet collapsed and was supporting the twisted safe door.'See that kinda – jam – oozin' out under the door? Nitro's moccasin's there an' his foot's still in it. He's done his last job for us, I reckon.'

Kane grunted after a cursory glance. 'Grab them bags before thay catch fire and let's get outta here.'

Two men started gathering the bags – at least eight, hopefully ten, while the others stepped past the wrecked counters where two clerks lay dazed, one bleeding from a cut in his temple. In the customer area eight townsfolk were sprawled about amidst splintered counters and shelves and piles of scattered papers. Most were groaning, not badly injured. A couple were too woozy to do anything but lie there staring dull-eyed, ears ringing. The front half-glass doors hung askew, shattered almost beyond recognition.

In the street, traffic was in chaos: a flatbed wagon had overturned, the team still hitched and whinnying wildly, pawing and snorting as they tried to get free. The passengers were sitting in the street, dazed. Store windows opposite had disintegrated, goods spilling on to the boardwalks. Folk were running about, mostly towards the bank, but others who had been too close to the explosion, headed the other way.

'Judas! Here comes the Law!' bawled a masked man with red hair showing under his hat, pointing to three men charging down the middle of the street. The sheriff, Tim Blood, carried a long-barrelled Greener, his two deputies clutched rifles across their chests, ready for action. 'Hell's teeth! It's Blood hisself!'

'Well, bid him welcome!' bawled Kane, moving to the front. 'You men, *move!*' he threw over his shoulder, then crouched by the hanging door. 'Mornin', Blood! Here's some breakfast for you! Got plenty of salt in it!'

In his excitement at getting a shot at his hated enemy, he pulled both triggers at once, and the rock salt whistled and fanned only halfway across the street.

But the charge of shot slammed into the rainbutt the sheriff had dived behind, smashing in several staves, water gushing.

'You always was too excitable, Kane!' The long barrelled Greener blasted in two heavy shots that rocked the big-chested lawman on his heels with recoil.

The sagging door above Kane shattered and collapsed in a shower of splintered wood and flying glass shards. 'I'll have twenty men surrounding you in a few minutes! End of the trail for you, Kane, you murdering son of a bitch!'

He must have reloaded fast because the Greener thundered and more of the already half-demolished doorway disintegrated. Rifles cracked in a ragged volley, pocking the front of the bank building, ricochets snarling.

'Hell, boss, there's men runnin' down this way from every-damn-where! They got us cold!' There was panic in the redhead's voice. Kane noted the fact for later.

He backed into the bank proper, turned and looked at the dazed and frightened survivors, saw a woman with long blonde curls blinking and shaking her head as she started to come out of her daze. Her dress was faded but mostly clean, now ripped in a couple of places from flying debris. One shoulder was bleeding and she favoured this arm as she instinctively tried to adjust her small hat that was askew on the long pin, hanging now from the tangled locks.

Kane strode across and grabbed her by the good shoulder, yanking her roughly to her feet. She cried out in pain and he held her easily, raked his steely eyes

9

around, 'Grab a couple more of these law-abidin' citizens! *C'mon! Hurry it up*! They got one helluva send-off waitin' for us.'

Another woman, with a little girl, crying as she clutched at her mother's dress, was dragged upright by the redheaded bandit. Two other robbers hauled up a fat, well-to-do-looking man in pin-striped trousers, with a flowered vest under a broadcloth coat and shoved him towards the door, a shotgun's hot barrels rammed against his flabby neck.

'No! No! – I have money! – I can pay. . . !'

A narrow-shouldered robber laughed, shook the terrified man.' You dummy! We've already got whatever money you had in this bank! Get in front where you can stop a bullet for me!'

Kane lined up his hostages at the doorway and the shooting from across the street stopped. Two more shots were fired by the outlaws and one citizen tumbled on to the boardwalk, writhing as he clutched at his side.

'Hold it!' bawled Kane. Then addressed the sheriff. 'Blood! See 'em? Take a good look. This is the best condition you'll see 'em in, you try to stop us leavin'! I have to spell it out for you?'

'No! You damn killer! But you harm any one of them! At least let the kid go!'

'Uh-uh, you family men'll hang back if you know she's along with Mommy! Only thing is, she'll be riding in front of me on my hoss! I go down, she goes with me. Savvy? Now, we got some negotiatin' to do?'

There was a brief silence and then Blood called, 'What's there to negotiate? I wouldn't trust your word if

10

you had wings and a halo!'

Kane chuckled. 'I'm tryin'! But don't look like I'll be too successful, so maybe I'll go t'other way: be a real bad bastard and see if I can do a deal with Old Nick!'

'You goin' or fixin' on havin' me send over breakfast?'

'Well – got me an appetite, I gotta admit – but I reckon I can wait a spell. Throw out your guns, then step out into the middle of the street. *Come on*! Every one of you upstandin' citizens! Ladies, too! Get out where we can see you, or your population's gonna drop, one by one. . . .'

He nodded and two of his men sent shots slamming into a storefront over the other side and soon there was a small crowd gathered in the middle of Main, men and women of all ages, pressing tightly together for comfort. No doubt other citizens were watching from behind locked doors of clapboard houses within viewing range – but no one stepped out or tried to intervene.

Tim Blood was nearest the bank, his sheriff's star glinting in the early sunlight. 'Turn loose them folk, Kane, and I'll come in their place.'

Kane laughed briefly. 'Big brave Blood, huh? But you'd be no good – I'd be tempted to kill you!'

Blood looked a bit pale now as he realized Kane's hate for him could well be demonstrated by a charge of buckshot right now. He lifted his hands slowly, shoulder-high, and his voice had a little tremor in it as he said to the others, 'Don't do nothin' foolish! Just obey him and you'll be all right.'

11

'That's good advice, folks,' Kane said, suddenly grabbing the crying little girl and swinging her up on to the big chestnut gelding one of his men had brought around for him, together with the other getaway mounts.

They all mounted quickly and Kane snapped at the child who began to scream and struggle now, reaching out towards her distraught mother.

'Quiet, kid, or I'll drown you in the hoss trough as we ride by!' He glared at the horrified mother. 'Tell her to shut up or I'll do what I said!'

The woman was draped over the saddle of another robber's horse and, her face reddened in that position, pleaded with the little girl to stay quiet. . . . '*Mommy's riding along with you, sweetheart! Just be quiet please, and everything'll be all right.*'

Kane started forward then stopped, his men hauling rein, too, puzzled.

'Blood, you folk don't look too happy clustered together out there. Mebbe you're too hot, jammed-up like that. Tell you what, I'll show you just how considerate I am.' He glanced up at the climbing sun, lifted a hand to shade his eyes. 'Sure is gonna be a hot one, you folk'll be better without them hot clothes, I reckon.'

The outlaws swiftly exchanged looks, their eyes crinkling above their bandanna masks as they smiled, a couple chuckling: Kane sure had a warped sense of humour!

'Good idea, boss!'

'Yeah. C'mon, folks! Peel 'em off!'

'Ya-hooooooo! Hey, blondie, you need a hand. . . ?'

12

'Man-oh-man!'

'You mean man-oh-*woman*!'

The townsfolk were shuffling about, aghast, no one yet attempting to remove any garment.

'Hurry 'em up,' growled Kane.

His men spurred forward, a couple loosing off shots into the air, others leaning from their saddles and ripping ladies' blouses, knocking off hats. One young woman was flung into the muddy pool made by the water draining from the buckshot-shattered rain butt.

'By God, Kane!' Tim Blood could barely speak, choked up with fury. The other men began cussing, never mind the women's tender ears.

But it didn't change anything. Kane drew his sixgun and slammed two shots into the air, and when he had everyone's attention, he lifted the still struggling, bawling little girl up by one arm. She screamed louder as she writhed.

He rode down by the horse trough, changed his grip to the child's ankle and suspended her over the scummy water upside down. Her hysterical mother collapsed in a dead faint.

'I'm lowering this kid down to the water, just a leetle bit at a time. Longer you take to disrobe, closer she comes to drowning. So, you good folks've got this sweet l'il child's life in your hands. Savvy?'

'You're dead, Kane!' screamed Blood in frustration. 'You hear me! Dead!'

'I hear you.' Kane lifted his sixgun and sighted on the sheriff who stiffened, blood draining from his face, convinced he was a breath away from dying.

'Blood – you got a choice. Step clear and strip down to

your lousy hide, right out where we can all see you, then get on tippy-toes and give us a twirl-an'-a-whirl. Savvy?' The mocking voice suddenly hardened and the hammer snapped to full cock. 'You got about two seconds, then, after I shoot you, I'll pick someone else until you all *do like I say! Which is: get them goddam clothes off!*'

The sheriff looked like he would just as soon die of a heart attack, but he tore off his shirt with trembling hands and then unbuckled his trousers belt.

Slowly, the others followed suit. . . .

Ten minutes later the Scattergun Gang cleared town, whooping and hollering with all of their hostages – including the now quietly-sobbing child, and armsful of the citizens' clothes. In the middle of Main, the buck-naked group were milling about haphazardly, trying to snatch up any piece of uncollected clothing to cover themselves. Some were even unwilling to stoop down to retrieve a garment: instead, hunkering and huddling, hoping no lecherous eyes were raking their pale flesh.

The sheriff was silent, standing there, arms straight down at his sides, seemingly uncaring about his state of nudity now. But there was a smouldering in his eyes as he watched the Scattergun Gang's dust cloud. . . .

There was lots of pale flesh to see: well-dressed citizens now revealing their flabbiness and sagging stomach muscles – revealing *all.*

A fight broke out between two men – one accusing the other of ogling his wife. Then two of the women began punching each other, the older one claiming the 'hussy' whose face she had just slapped had tried to 'touch' her husband inappropriately.

'Honey,' gritted the young woman, rubbing her stinging face, 'If I don't know how to touch a man *appropriately* by now I'll walk to the Memorial Park and lay me down under the she-oak and any man who wants to follow can come right along and join the queue, and it won't cost him a red cent!'

'Whore!'

'And havin' more fun that you ever will, you old hag! Hell, I can see the icicles on you from here, you're so damn frigid!'

It erupted into a lot of name-calling, a few more slaps, and lots of uneasy ribald laughter from the men, until one woman pointed towards the nether regions of a husky, well-built man.

'By Godfrey! How could *he* father them two six-footer sons of his with – *that*! – I've seen bigger on a statue of a baby cherub!'

That was when an all-in brawl erupted that even the sheriff couldn't break-up . . . not that he tried. He was past caring. The only thing he had on his mind now was getting Scattergun Kane in his sights . . . with his own finger on the trigger.

But, by that time, the Scattergun Gang were heading into the foothills with the money, *and* their hostages.

Even Tim Blood in his present state had to admit that the Scattergun Gang had won this round.

He silently swore that he would spend the rest of his life if need be, hunting down these men, and he wouldn't be satisfied until every last one was dead.

'No one hands me a raw deal like this and lives to tell about it!'

CHAPTER 2

END OF THE WORLD

Josh McCall thought his spine was being rammed up through the top of his head as the wild-eyed, foam-spitting smoke came down from its buckjump on four legs, each as stiff and unbending as a ramrod. His nose started bleeding again.

He grunted, feeling every ounce of breath forced out between his teeth as they clashed together: he tasted blood. His neck promised to snap if he didn't grip tighter with knees and hands, preventing the violent jarring of the riotous animal beneath him. No time! The horse was already into another bone-cracking roll, lunging at the lodgepole rails of the corral fence, determined to break his leg.

McCall knew when it was time to quit and had one leg over the saddlehorn when he lost his grip. He found

16

out what it was like for a man to fly – briefly – and to land without any means of softening the process. Hoofs slashed down inches from his thudding head and he let instinct take command, rolled under the fence, coming to rest on his belly, face in the dust.

The horse continued to take out its wicked temper on the ground and fence, snorting, whinnying, arching its back, kicking hind legs straight out with a force that would have launched McCall into the next county if they had connected. He got to his knees, clinging to the lower rails, spitting dust mixed with blood.

'Go on! Get rid of that bile, you useless jughead!' he gritted, coughing and spitting some more. *Man! Did his bones ache! And his belly felt like it had been torn out of his body, his spine tied in a hangman's knot. . . .*

The smoke snorted, stomped, jumped around, glaring at him, nostrils twitching, mad eyes seeming to be figuring some way to get at him.

Then there was a shot and the animal reared, had time to paw the air briefly, before smashing down on to its side, legs kicking, blood oozing from a bullet hole in the huge head.

Momentarily stunned, McCall blinked, then turned quickly, pulling himself upright.

A small band of dusty men sat jaded mounts, facing him. Each held a gun: a rifle or sixgun or shotgun. The man out front had a Winchester that was smoking and he used the barrel to point to the now dead horse in the corral.

'Only thing to do with a devil-bitch like that,' Scattergun Kane rasped.'Likely to've killed you anyway,

17

even if you'd managed to quiet it down – just wait its chance.'

McCall's blue eyes went to the post where his sixgun rig hung, the sun glinting from the brass shells: there were more empty loops than full. He knew he could never reach it before this big, dangerous-looking man shot him, so he faced Kane squarely, saying,

'Like to decide if I'm gonna kill one of my broncs myself, mister! I spent a lot of time working with that critter.'

'Saved you some hurt, you dumb bastard, don't you see that?' Kane stood in his stirrups, looking beyond the small working corral to the big one, ten yards closer to the brush where there were a dozen bareback horses milling restlessly. 'See you already broke some. We'll pick out what we need. Trade you these for 'em.'

He casually gestured to the jaded, head-hanging knee-knocked mounts he and his men sat astride.

McCall stiffened. 'The hell you will.'

'Oh, we will, friend. Hell don't come into it . . . Red, you and Slats start cuttin'-out some likely broncs. Bring a couple spares. Never know when we might need 'em – or how far behind Blood is.'

McCall frowned. 'Posse after you?'

Kane sighed and shook his head. 'Now why'd you have to go an' say that? Dammit, mister, I was about to ride on and let you live – dunno why, just a whim, I guess – but now you just raked my craw! I hate smart-mouthed sons of bitches pokin' their nose into my business. So you can go to hell. *Adios*!'

McCall started to throw himself aside but Kane was

18

too fast. The rifle came up and he triggered one-handed. McCall's thick yellow hair lifted violently and his head snapped back as he crashed into the corral fence, legs folding. He went down gracefully enough, and there was blood masking his face before his knees struck the ground. The jar flung his body forward. One arm slipped between the rails and hung him up there, spine bent, body otherwise limp, blood dripping first on to the wood, then the ground.

Kane spat, turned to the others. 'Move!'

As the men started towards the holding corrals, a middle-aged man with a slanted mouth, pointed to the hogback.

'Trace of smoke over yonder, Scattergun. Might be a house.'

'Could be – I'm partial to some home cookin' and I ain't had any in a coon's age. Get the saddles on the fresh mounts and we'll go check it out.'

It must be the fires of hell, blasting heat like that!

It was only a half-acknowledged thought in his thundering skull but he grunted as something like a vice clamped on his upper left arm and shook him.

'Hey! Hey, c'mon – you McCall?'

The voice was harsh and his eyes flickered, the lids sticky. A damp rag wiped away the blood and he had to blink for half a minute before the redness cleared and he looked up into the stubbled face of a man wearing a battered Derby hat.

'That's it – that's better.' The man turned his head, looking strangely reddish – *glow from hell's fires, maybe?* –

and called, 'He's with us, Sheriff. Hasn't yet admitted to being McCall, but he's alive.'

'He gonna stay that way, doc?' Sheriff Tim Blood hunkered down beside the medic and reached out to push some of the blood-stiffened yellow hair back from McCall's forehead. 'We ain't met, but I've heard you were workin' the fringes of the dustbowl, breakin' horses from the foothills, McCall. I'm Tim Blood, sheriff of Jacksboro.'

The wounded man cleared his throat and it hurt to talk. 'Josh McCall. Anyone got some water?'

The doctor uncapped a canteen and held the neck to his mouth, spilling some over McCall's chin. 'Take a good long drink. Seems to me you been lying in the sun a goodly spell. It's an hour past sundown now.'

McCall pushed the canteen away, coughed a little, glanced up, eyes wild. He struggled to rise but it was no effort for the doctor to hold him down.

'Damn! It's late. . . !'

'Easy, man!'

'My wife! She'll be worried. . . . Got to get back to her. Ranch house is over yonder rise and. . . .' His words ran off and he looked more closely at their faces. 'Wh-what is it? What's wrong. . . ?'

'You take it easy, like Doc says, feller,' Tim Blood told him. 'No. no! Come on! Just lie there a spell – Who shot you anyway?'

McCall had to think hard, frowning. He rubbed a hand across his scarred and blood-sticky forehead. 'Someone called Kane. Shot my horse first, then me.'

Blood was tensed now and McCall looked past him,

saw other men moving about, horses being cared for.

'Kane wasn't alone?'

'Uh. . . ? No. six or seven men with him. Rough as cobs. Mean sonuvers – He was worried you were close behind him. With a posse. . . .'

Blood nodded, face grim. 'Scattergun Kane's bunch. Blew our bank apart and got away with more'n thirty-thousand in cash. Left a lot of folk dead. Took hostages and they. . . .'

The doctor coughed and shook his head slightly at the lawman.

'Yeah, gave us a hard time, 'the sheriff said.'We had trouble trailin' 'em. They been riding owlhoot for years. Know all the trails around here. But we kept after 'em.'

McCall nodded slowly, still rubbing his forehead, looking worried. 'You must've, their mounts were jaded. They took my herd, the ones I'd broke to saddle. Was getting ready to add that smoke to 'em and drive 'em to town or mebbe Fort Garnett, we need some money. House's only partly built and I got to give my wife a decent home before winter and. . . .'

Again he saw that exchange of looks between the medic and the lawman as he gestured to the rise.

'What's happened. . . ? My wife, Rosa. . . . She OK?'

Blood glanced at Doc Perry but the medico threw it squarely into his lap. 'Well, we – I sent a man over the hill but he ain't brought us any news yet – You feel up to sittin' a saddle by mornin', we'll go check on your place.'

''By morning? The hell with that! We go check

tonight!' McCall flung off their efforts this time and stumbled and staggered half upright. One leg buckled but the doctor steadied him.

'Son, you go easy. You were lucky. That shot had been a hair lower, it'd taken the top of your skull off. As it is, you're going to have one helluva headache for a few days – may even suffer memory loss. . . .'

'I can handle whatever comes, Doc – It's not me I'm worried about.' He flicked his cold blue eyes to the sheriff. 'Why'd you send a man over the rise. . . ? I mean, what made you do that? My house can't be seen from here.'

Blood hesitated. 'Smoke. One of the boys thought they saw smoke rising.' He added quickly: 'Like from a chimney, so we thought there must be a house close by.'

'And the man ain't come back! The hell're doing sitting here, Blood? Send someone after him, find out what he's found! Better still, go yourself – and take me with you!'

Doc Perry held McCall's shoulders, feeling the muscles and tendons there like steel cables, the man was so tense. He nodded to the sheriff.

'I think that's a good idea, Tim. All this agitation and – uncertainty – won't do Mr McCall any good.'

Blood sighed. 'All right. We're all movin' over there anyway. . . . Barney! Come lend McCall a hand till he gets his wits about him properly. We're goin' over the hogback.'

It was no easy ride in the dark over the rise, which was not only steep but badly rutted from past heavy rains.

Long past. . . . And McCall knew well before they topped-out what he was going to see.

He could smell the acrid woodsmoke, *taste* it, knew it wasn't from any kitchen stove.

This was the smell of a wooden building that had been destroyed by fire.

His head was spinning and he clung tightly to the saddlehorn, reins wrapped around his wrists so that they cut grooves in the sun-dark flesh.

Blood had been trying to keep his distance but saw the rancher's pale face now as McCall turned towards him. 'Tell me,' he said quietly.

'I dunno. Our man came back and said he'd seen the house from the crest. That – that it had been burned and there were dead animals in the yard. . . . He rode on down, just before you started to come round. I dunno nothin' else.'

McCall gave him a blistering look. 'Thanks a lot, you son of a bitch!'

He spurred his horse ahead and Blood called, 'I was tryin' to make it easier for you!'

McCall suddenly reined down, hipped in the saddle, almost tumbling from it. 'Kane never had no hostages with him here?'

'No.'

'You said he took hostages. What happened to 'em?'

'Look, McCall, take it easy, we'll ride over and see what. . . .'

McCall wrenched the horse around and, obviously still feeling none too secure in the saddle, spurred away, hit the downslope and rode recklessly towards the dimly-seen outline of the gutted house.

The dog, Rosa's red setter, and the marmalade cat, who had favoured McCall himself, were dead in the yard. Both had been blasted by a shotgun, not much left of them.

There was no door standing, only part of the north wall, the west one tumbled in, but charred, and still smouldering. The bedroom was underneath somewhere. He dismounted and his legs buckled so he had to grab the saddle for support. Blood walked up and steadied him but McCall wrenched his arm away from the man.

A man came out of the charred mess, glanced at McCall and faced the sheriff.

'Looks like they smashed everythin' up before they set it alight, Tim. Had 'emselves a time of it.'

Blood frowned and cut in quickly, glancing at McCall. 'This is Josh McCall, Paddy – it was his place.'

'Oh. Sorry you had to find it this way, McCall.'

The wounded man nodded jerkily, swallowed, steeled himself. 'Any – bodies?'

Paddy licked his lips and shook his head.

'Then she could've got out!' There was false hope making McCall's voice suddenly loud. 'That's it! She got out and she's hiding in the brush! Frightened by all you men – thinking maybe you're part of the bunch who did this. . . .'

Blood looked away and then McCall turned to the man who had been in amongst the ruins. 'I guess not. But you think there's a chance she might've made it?'

'Well, no sign of a body. I guess, well, mebbe Kane

24

and his men. . . .'

'Paddy! Shut up!' snapped Blood and McCall's face was white, hard-planed in the dim light.

'Damn you, Blood! I asked you a while back – *what happened to the hostages Kane's bunch took?*'

The sheriff looked uncomfortable. 'We found 'em along the trail, where he'd left 'em.'

Josh McCall stared silently, then, his voice barely audible, asked, 'Alive. . . ?'

Sheriff Tim Blood stared back, mighty uncomfortable. Then shook his head briefly.

'Not a single one.'

Doc Perry grabbed McCall as the man swayed, glaring at the lawman.

But it was too late: McCall knew Rosa was already dead, or would be, long before they caught up with Kane's Scattergun Gang.

He may not be right at the end of the world here, but he figured if he raised up on to his toes he would see it clearly.

One great black emptiness – waiting for him.

CHAPTER 3

LONER

Josh McCall swiftly reloaded the smoking Colt as he stood with one foot on the bloody chest of the man he had just killed. He only had four cartridges left.

He looked around the red walls of the large, meandering canyon, but felt pretty certain there was no one else waiting: they'd just left this poor misguided son of a bitch at his feet to watch the backtrail. Too bad he was dead – whatever information he had about Scattergun Kane's gang he took with him to hell. . . .

Mind, it had been a close go.

It was three weeks since Kane had left him for dead back at his ranch and Rosa had disappeared. It had been a long, long trail and his head wound had given him a lot of pain but was easing now. Tim Blood, seething at the humiliation he had experienced at Kane's hands on Main Street had finally driven his posse into rebellion as the weeks passed without any real result.

They argued, cursed him, then scattered, returning to town and their families or businesses. Only McCall had stuck, and when Blood finally admitted defeat, the sheriff had told him:

'Can't leave you deputized, McCall. You'll be on your own if you stick it out, lookin' for the bastards.'

'I work better alone.'

'You don't savvy what I mean. You'll have no official standing. You find Kane or some of his gang, run 'em down and then give 'em hell trying to find out what happened to your wife, well, the way the law looks at it, you'll be just as guilty of a crime as any of the Scattergun Gang.'

'I won't lose one minute's sleep over that.'

The sheriff sighed. 'OK, I've broken the law, too, workin' outside my jurisdiction. But there ain't much I can do to help if some hard-nosed Brazos sheriff decides to throw you in jail. You kill someone in cold blood and they'll likely hang you. Every lawman between here and the Territory is just as mean as Scattergun Kane – for different reasons. What they like to call "Law Of The Panhandle".'

McCall looked squarely at the lawman, nodded curtly. 'They can try and stop me. Try. *Adios*, Blood.'

He wheeled his mount, a dusty, spotted grey, and rode towards distant, misted hills.

'I can let you have a little extra ammunition!' Blood called after a pause.

McCall merely lifted a hand in acknowledgement and kept on riding . . . *impatient. Implacable.*

Two days later he picked up sign that belonged to

27

one of the horses Kane's men had stolen from him. None of the bunch was shod, and these hoofprints weren't either.

The trail led him into the red-walled canyon, snaking through the rear of Misery Mountain. It was officially known as 'Borthwick's Canyon', named after the Yankee commander who took Jacksboro in that big siege of '64.

But some smart-mouth local had said, 'You say "Horseshit Canyon"?'

' "*Borthwick's*" Canyon,' the land agent corrected him, with a half-smile.

'Well, "Horseshit" fits better – he was full of it!'

That got a laugh from the group who had gathered around the Land Agency and even the Agent himself smiled crookedly. He scratched an ear lobe.

'We-ell, have to agree with you, Daybreak. But you won't find your version printed on these new maps.'

He was right, but it didn't matter: everyone in the Panhandle referred to the place as 'Horseshit' Canyon. . . .

McCall had never been here before but had been planning a trip. A buffalo-runner had told him of big bunches of mustangs using this canyon: there were large waterholes and patches of good grass in hidden pockets.

But it seemed the man he was trailing knew it well enough to hide on top of an ochre-coloured wall with broken greyish streaks running across it horizontally.

As far as McCall could see there was no way up and the wall looked continuous. In any case, he was concentrating on the ground, leaning slightly to the left in the saddle, checking for hoofprints. Even though his headwound began to throb, pounding behind his eyes, he forced himself to stay in position, searching for a disturbance of the dust or gravel made by an unshod hoof.

He saw what looked like one – just as a rifle fired above him and the bullet *zipped* past his bent head, thudded into the ground, puffing dust. As he was already leaning that way, McCall let himself fall – regretting that he wasn't able to grab his rifle from the saddle boot.

But he lit on his shoulders, air blasting out of his lungs forcing him to grunt. He rolled in close to the base of the wall, tight as he could manage. The man above fired again, but he wasn't leaning far enough out over the edge and the bullet ploughed harmlessly into the trail, a couple of yards behind the now running horse.

McCall had his Colt in his hand now, watched the shadow of the rim, where the killer was holed-up: it was just touching the opposite wall. There was a slight movement, barely breaking into the skyline, slowly – and, it seemed, awkwardly.

He's stepping over the edge! Going to work along to that narrow foothold so he can see the base of this wall right here where I am. . . . Sonuver aims to get me.

'Likewise, killer!' he said aloud.

McCall rolled out into the trail and there, high above, was the bushwhacker, inching his way along this side of the rim, clinging like a fly, boot toes digging into some of those grey streaks of shale. It wasn't the hardest of rocks and just as McCall triggered two shots, the piece under the killer's right shoe broke away. He almost fell, body jarring as he clawed at the rim, legs swinging: the shots missed.

By the time McCall came up to his knees, the rifleman had thrown himself back over the edge and squirmed back on to the ridge. McCall's next shot also missed though rock chips were chewed out only inches from the man's body.

McCall lay there, in the trail, gun smoking, waiting for the killer's next move. *Yeah! Just as he hoped!*

The man saw McCall down there, on his back, a fine, tempting target. He thrust up to his knees, rifle at his shoulder, squeezed off a short volley that had McCall squirming and kicking up dust desperately as he lunged for the base of the wall again. The closer in he was the harder it would be for the killer to get at him.

Panting, trying to remember how many shots he had fired, he saw the man's shadow plainly now on the opposite wall. The fool was leaning way out over the rim. McCall's Colt came up and he gripped his right wrist firmly with his left hand, thumbed the hammer and put the last two bullets into the dry-gulcher.

He didn't make a sound on the way down, but he hit with a dull thud that told McCall he was not going to be in very good shape. . . .

That was when he went across and planted a boot over the man's bleeding chest wound. Wide, glazing eyes stared up at the rancher.

'Where's Kane?'

The man spat at him. It was unexpected and McCall

arched his eyebrows. 'Have it your way. One more time: where's Kane?'

He leaned his weight on his scuffed riding boot, the battered spur rowel chinging briefly. The man screamed and coughed up a lot of blood. McCall eased up the pressure a little. The killer's body convulsed once, like a bow loosing off an arrow. 'M – makin' for the – terr – terri—'

He couldn't finish the sentence and McCall stepped back, finished reloading his gun. The man was trying to say 'territory'. Land that would eventually become Oklahoma. But at this time it was known as the Cherokee Strip or Indian Territory, a land without Law, where every thief or killer who could make it found sanctuary, at least for a while. Some stayed permanently. Six feet under, or fodder for the coyotes.

McCall had figured that was where Kane would go to hole-up until things settled down some. He aimed to play a hunch, and check it out after first trying Horseshit Canyon.

But he should have accepted Blood's offer of ammunition. He took what was in the dead man's belt loops, but only got two shells from the rifle's magazine. He gazed up at the wall, wondering if he could find a way up there? But this outlaw looked like he had been running rough since the robbery in Jacksboro, so may not have any extra anyway. . . .

Food he didn't have to carry: he was used to hunting his own grub. But, for chasing down someone like Kane and his rannies, he needed plenty of ammunition. And reliable firearms.

So he would have to find a town and – *No!* Fort Garnett would be closer: he knew the commandant there, had sold him remounts and a few cattle for his troops last fall.

He might be able to give him some information about the forbidden Badman's Territory, too: he would need as much as he could gather if he aimed to stay alive in there.

And he did – he *wanted* to stay alive – at least long enough to find the Scattergun Gang and kill them one by one.

And, hopefully, learn exactly what had happened to Rosa. There hadn't been any trace of her since leaving his burned-out ranch.

Nothing.

It was the not-knowing that was eating at him.

He *felt* she was gone: he had to be honest with himself and admit there wasn't much chance she would survive for long at the hands of Kane's murderous gang.

But the worst thing he found, wasn't accepting that she was probably dead, it was that niggling, half-buried *hope* that she *could* be still alive!

He fought mighty hard to suppress the feeling. It wasn't that he wanted her to be dead – hell np! But he didn't know how long he could bear to live with the implied *possibility* that she might still be alive, only to find out, finally, she was dead, had been all along, prob-ably since a few hours after Kane had abducted her. . . .

But he would endure whatever hell he had to until he learned the truth.

He rowelled the spotted grey furiously in his hurry to

clear the canyon, the hoofbeats drumming a tattoo that, in his head, seemed to say,

Rose-uh! Rose-uh! Rose-uh!

Then, galloping – *Rosarosarosarosarosa.*

Fort Garnett, on the high bend of the Brazos River, was in a state of frantic activity when McCall rode his weary mount through the gates.

A three-wagon train was being loaded by cursing soldiers, in collarless, sweat-stained undershirts, dusty and dirty trousers held up by frayed army-issue suspenders. The men looked harassed and striding, swearing corporals and sergeants moved among them, urging them to more speed in the loading, always more speed. *At the double! At the double double!*

McCall's spotted grey plodded up near one of the redfaced non-coms, a sergeant named Darnley, and nudged his shoulder lightly.

'Who the blazes did that?' roared Darnley, rounding fast, eyes lifting to the dusty, unshaven man in the saddle, not recognizing him at first. 'Goddammittohell! You civilians were told ten thousand damn times to stay outta this area when we're gearin'-up for a field patrol! Now get the—' He stopped, frowning and squinting, wiping curved fingers across his furrowed brow and dashing sweat to the ground. 'God save us! Joshua McCall! We heard you were dead. . . .' His voice lowered abruptly and he cleared his throat. 'The word was your good woman – Rosa? – had been taken hostage by that murderous bastard, Scattergun Kane. . . .'

'Murderous bastard is right, Gavin. They left a man to bushwhack me but I was lucky enough to spot him. Kane himself tried to shoot me but I guess I have a thick skull.'

Darnley had a face like the knotty end of a tree root and he grinned, showing big teeth with at least one gap. 'Oh, sure, I know the kinda "luck" you use! What you make for yourself. Anyway, it's good it is to see you.' He pinched the nostrils of his large, pitted nose. 'Phew! I think mebbe your hoss needs a good curry-combin'. I'll fix it. An'why don't you dunk yourself in our bath-barrel under yonder *ramada*? Water ain't but a day or so old. . . .'

McCall half-smiled. 'Didn't know you were so tactful, Gavin. . . . Yeah. I'll take up your offer. But I have to see the Major . . . he in the fort?'

Darnley pulled a face. 'Have your bath first,' he advised. 'An', if you got a change of shirt. . . .'

McCall nodded. 'In one of those moods, is he?' He gestured to the preparations. 'Big patrol?'

'Aye. Into the Territory.'

McCall tensed. '*Indian* Territory?'

'Aye. That Scattergun gang's been rampagin' across the north here. Loco as a pack of wolves with rabies. They even hit a small Injun hunting camp, scalped the braves. Must be blood-lettin' crazy.' He saw McCall's face straighten and awkwardly wiped a hand across his nostrils. 'Er. Well, they're sendin' us in, seein' as we're Federal-funded. The word is to clean the place out. Kane and his killers are first priority, then a general purge.'

'Mebbe my timing's good then. It's where I want to go.' *And I hope Rosa's survived. . . !*

'Aaah! Well, now, you be on your best behaviour when you see the Major or he's likely to kick you over the stockade wall.'

'Doesn't like his orders. . . ?'

Darnley shook his head ponderously. 'There's a couple US Marshals already in there, undercover, and, this is what don't set in the Major's craw too good: if we come across one, the *Marshal*'s the laddie to have all the say.'

McCall whistled softly, his lips dry and cracked. 'No wonder the Major's upset – but how come?'

'Marshals've been runnin' a deal in there for a few weeks. Almost ready to move on the bunch they're after, the crew they think are helpin' that European someone brought in to kill the President. You hear about that? While the President was visitin' Tucumari, for their fifti-eth anniversary or somethin'. Seems he was born there. Feller they call The Spider wounded him but got away. No one knows what he looks like but the Marshals've had some luck and got a lead. They don't like the idea we might spook their quarry – they want him bad in Washington – need to find out who hired him. . . .'

'You quite finished disseminating Army information to every drifter who passes through, Sergeant Darnley?'

Big and tough as he was, Darnley paled and snapped to attention, almost knocking his sun-faded cap off as he saluted the man in Major's uniform under the shade of the *ramada* a few feet away.

'Sorry, sir! But, underneath all that grime you'll find

Josh McCall an' as he's. . . .'

The major, a medium-sized man, was leaning over the peeled lodgepole railing, peering at McCall, who smiled wide enough to show some of his stained teeth.

'It's me, Grant. Looking for help to locate Rosa. . . .'

Major Grant Usher lifted a hand to his droopy moustache, then gestured for McCall to dismount and follow him into his office. He turned his battle-hardened eyes on to the grinning Darnley who had been feeling relieved – briefly. He scratched one ear briefly, then snapped,

'You get yourself into a set of fatigues, Sergeant – and lend those men a hand. An example will do more than all the cuss-words in Texas – I believe you know the lot?'

Darnley, deflated, saluted more slowly this time.

'Yessir – I – I think mebbe I've just figured out a couple new ones. . . .'

'Try 'em out on that wagon gang then,' snapped the officer and led the way into his office.

It was cool, but untidy in the office. Usher had to move piles of papers in order to find the key to the cupboard where the whiskey was kept. As he set a full glass in front of McCall he wrinkled his nose.

'We'll make this brief: Heard about Kane takin' Rosa. Mighty sorry about that. Knew he'd head for the Territory. I've been houndin' Washington and they've finally decided to act, but only because some square-head or frog-eater tried to shoot the President. They say he missed only by a hair, too, when the President jerked his head to dodge a bluetail fly! Army got word he might've run to the Territory to hide out so we're

36

making the proper response, for whatever good it'll do.'

McCall sipped the whiskey, wincing a little. It was good liquor but it was a long, long time since he had tasted any alcohol.

'Grant, I need to come with you. Or I need some kinda paper that'll give me authority in the Territory.'

'Easy, Josh! I can't issue anything like that!'

'OK, I'll go anyway, but it'd be easier, and safer, if I had something in writing.'

'Or more dangerous. Suppose one of the local residents finds the paper on you? You'd be lucky to live another five minutes.'

'I've thought of that. But I don't want to be shot down by a US Marshal or the damn US Cavalry. Having a document won't guarantee it won't happen, but I'd feel better if I had something to show. And as soon as I get Kane and free Rosa I'll be back in Texas before you can spit.'

Major Usher had downed his first drink and poured a second, gesturing for McCall to help himself, but the rancher just took another sip. A small one.

'Is there any news on the gang?' he asked tentatively. 'Apart from attacking an Indian camp?'

The major looked at him steadily. 'I was going to say "no", because what we have isn't "news". No, wait, let me finish, Kane's laid a trail of death right along the Brazos and now we know for sure he's headed for the Territory. It's only coincidence that he's going there just as Washington decides to clean up the place.'

'Kane's too wild to let that worry him. Take more

than an army to flush him out. Or less.'

'Mmmm – an army mightn't be able to do it, being so prominent in its actions, giving him plenty of warning where they're operating.' He paused. 'But a loner might be able to slip in close. That what you're telling me?'

'He might be on the lookout for me, but if your men are tearing up the countryside, you'll grab a lot of his attention. I ought to be able to slip under his guard while he's lookin' the other way.'

Usher smiled crookedly. 'You might've had some trouble with rotgut scramblin' your thinking a couple years ago, but there's nothing wrong with your grey matter now.'

McCall shrugged. 'Rosa kept me from drinkin' myself to death, you know that. She turned me right around and we were married last fall, The money from the beef and remounts I sold you helped us set up the spread near Misery Mountain, Grant, I'm obliged to you for that. But I need this favour.'

Sober-faced, Usher nodded. 'I wasn't looking for thanks, but Kane's come out of nowhere and tore your life apart. Don't get me wrong, but I wasn't sure you'd be sober.'

McCall shook his head.'That other time was different. Now, if I want to find Rosa, I've got to stay sober. You still haven't told me what you've heard about Kane.'

Usher sighed, looked at the low level of whiskey in his glass but decided to leave it: McCall must have a mighty powerful iron will not to grab the bottle by the neck and swamp it down, with the worry he was carrying about Rosa: so no use giving it a nudge in the wrong direction. . . .

'Josh, it seems that Kane's travelling with a couple of women.'

McCall sat up so fast he spilled what was left of his drink. He set the glass down and absently wiped his hand on his trail-dusted shirt, watching Usher's face.

'A *couple*! Was one Rosa?'

Usher sighed. 'I don't know, Josh. That's what I meant when I said there was no real news. Just that Kane's got two women with him now.'

'One with red-gold hair like she has, Grant?'

McCall was standing now and Usher said quietly, 'Far as I know, both women have black hair. Very black. . . . Sorry, *amigo*.'

He watched the blood drain slowly from Josh McCall's begrimed and gaunted face.

CHAPTER 4

BADLANDS

'Mack? What's the rest of it?'

'Short for "McCrae", Callum McCrae.'

'No wonder you like Mack better, and what're you doin' here, in my bailiwick?'

McCall, trail-weary and looking tougher than ever with gritty stubble, a torn shirt sleeve and a fading bruise under his left eye, leaned on the saddlehorn and looked steadily at the man slouched against a rock at the entrance to the large cave. He held a sawed-off shotgun in his left hand – pointing groundward now – but the grip would allow him to swing it up, ready for action in the blink of an eye. If McCall had come to the right place (and he had followed his informant's directions closely) this man had to be the one called 'Rocca'.

'Lookin' to lay low.'

'Uh-huh – and why would that be?'

McCall hesitated, tried to appear furtive. Looking

nervous was easy enough, but the other. However, he must have managed it, because Rocca smiled crookedly when McCall didn't answer right away.

'Consider yourself among friends here, till I tell you otherwise.'

'You hear about the stage hold-up at Fat Man Gap? Couple weeks ago. . . ?'

'The Butterfield Line? You sayin' that was you?'

'I pulled it.' There was silence amongst the three men watching him closely, hands tightening on their guns now.

The man with the shotgun shook his head, lifting the weapon. 'That was Waco Jansen. He went through here a week back like he was saddlin' a twister. Hardly stopped long enough to reload his guns. *He* pulled that deal, and had a full-blown posse after him. . . . Now, you say *you* did the job?'

McCall didn't move, merely smiled. 'We-ell – mebbe I heard someone mention the hold-up and thought it'd sound good if I claimed to've done it. Don't want to talk about why I'm on the dodge . . . I am. Just leave it at that, huh?'

'Gimme a hint,' said Rocca, unsmiling, resting the gun across his chest now.

McCall sighed. 'OK. Ridin' a hoss that didn't belong to me, I got to the Brazos, when the jughead baulked in mid-river, left me sittin' there like a fly on a wedding cake. A posse I'd been dodging caught up. We traded a little lead. Two posse men went down . . . I only seen one get back up.'

They looked at him more closely now and slowly the

41

shotgunner asked, 'You bring that posse here with you?'

'No. One of the men I shot was the sheriff. Last I seen the posse was heading back to where they come from. More interested in getting him to a sawbones than chasing me.'

'You say!'

'Think it's the first posse I've had to out-run?' McCall sounded belligerent and Rocca's eyes narrowed.

'Don't push your luck, feller.'

'Hell, I've been pushing it for weeks. You want me to ride on, say so, I ain't begging you to stay.'

'Aaah, simmer down, we gotta check you out. Light 'n' eat, we'll talk some more.'

It wasn't an invitation delivered with good grace. Rocca's shotgun barrels casually lifted and covered McCall as he dismounted stiffly and loosened the cinch strap on the dappled grey. 'Haven't et for two days – so hope you got plenty of vittles.'

'You'll eat as much or as little as we care to give you,' growled a man in baggy clothes, tall, lean and mean. He had sandy-coloured hair and McCall learned he went by the name of Rusty. 'And you'll like it . . . or lump it.'

Rocca grinned and spat, putting the shotgun over his shoulder now, turned and led the way into the cave.

'I need something to put cash in my pockets as well as grub in my belly,' McCall said. 'I can handle a gun and I'm good at tracking as well as covering-up a trail. . . .'

'We'll talk about that while we eat.'

The men watched him with various degrees of suspicion. Two got up, chewing on some tough, charred meat and went outside, not speaking, as McCall reached for a hunk of the same unknown meat, sawed off a thick slice with a knife with a dirty blade. But, chewing, listening carefully, he could hear the creak of leather and rummaging at the cave mouth: they were searching his gear.

He shifted around where he was sitting, making sure his elbows were clear of the rock walls and also used the move to cover his right hand tilting his holster to the best position for a fast draw.

'You know your way around the Territory?' Rocca asked.

'Never had to run this far before.'

'Next time, don't kill a posse man – I'd like to be damn sure that posse didn't follow you in here.'

McCall shrugged. 'I already said they didn't.'

'They *better* not!' growled Rusty.

'If it bothers you, I'll be on my way come morning. That's if it's OK to stop over tonight?'

'Polite, ain't he?' commented the sandy-haired man chewing noisily.

They all looked up as the two men came back from searching McCall's gear. The one with the scarred, broken nose, Nate Denby, shook his head curtly. The other said, 'He could be Jesus makin' the Second Coming for all the identification we found.'

'You're thinking of my brother,' McCall said with a wry grin, but it didn't soften the suspicious faces. 'Learned a long time ago never to carry anything with my name on it.' They continued to stare. 'Just call me Mack, I'll be outta your hair by morning.'

'Or sooner,' said Rusty, the rawhide one. Hard, unblinking eyes nailed McCall: the man seemed to be looking for trouble.

McCall sighed and grimaced as he swallowed a mouthful of bitter coffee. He stood slowly. 'You oughta think about firin' your cook before he poisons you,' he told Rocca.

'*I'm* the cook!' snapped Rusty, jumping up. McCall had already figured that as the man was surrounded by recently used utensils, a smear of flour on his lantern jaw.

'Mister, I'll show you how to boil water before I leave if you want. . . . Won't make you a cook, but it's a start.'

That was enough for Rusty. He was cursing even as he went for his gun, but froze with it halfway drawn. He found himself facing a rock-steady Colt in McCall's right hand, the hammer cocked, The eyes that studied him were cold and committed. . . . It was Rusty's move, now.

Not a man in the cave seemed to breathe. Their eyes flicked from one to the other: they could all see that Rusty knew he was a dead man if he pushed this. He might have a fiery temper, but in the face of that gun waiting to send him on his way to Hell, he found himself cooling down right smartly. He let his big, bony hand drop away from his gun butt, spread both arms well out to his sides.

'This time!' he gritted, unable to let it go completely.

'Anything you say.' McCall returned the sixgun to his holster almost as fast as he had drawn it. *He'd accomplished what he'd wanted to: now they knew he could handle a*

44

gun – and, more importanly, was ready to shoot it.

Rocca squinted at McCall. 'I could use you.'

'Not just me.' McCall's eyes gestured at the others.

Rocca grinned crookedly. 'Sassy, huh? Well, gun speed like that gives you certain – privileges. But, wouldn't push it too far, was I you . . . these are good men.'

'Ah, let him go, Rock,' growled Rusty. 'Don't trust him. Man can draw like that could as well be a undercover lawman as someone on the dodge. Word's goin'round they's a Marshal in the Territory somewheres – wears his badge pinned to his underwear, they say.'

McCall smiled crookedly. 'Let's me out, I don't wear any. Rocca, I ain't gonna thank you for the sloppy grub, but it's the sentiment that counts, I guess.'

Rocca laughed out loud. 'Hear that, Rusty. . . ? Hey, Mack, listen: stay a spell. What really brought you to the Territory? Might be able to help you.'

'And yourself.' Rocca shrugged, spreading his hands. McCall did some fast thinking: lay it out before these hardcases and throw in a little sweetening, and maybe he could get a lot of help . . . which he could sure use in these badlands. Deciding, he said, '*Why* I'm on the dodge, don't matter. You know The Scattergun Gang?'

A brief silence. Then, Rocca spoke: 'Kane's bunch? They'd be too rough for you, Mack. No one wants anythin' to do with 'em. They come into the Territory and, after what they done in Jacksboro, place'll be crawlin' with soldiers and posses, not to mention bounty hunters.' He squinted at McCall, dropped his eyes to the holstered sixgun. 'Ah! Now I begin to see!'

'You only think you do, but you're on the right track. They've got eighteen thousand bucks bounty riding 'em right now, more'n half of what they stole in Jacksboro.' He lied calmly, easily. 'But they say it's the dead the gang left behind that pushed the bounty up, not what they stole.'

Rusty snorted. 'Hogwash! They stripped the townsfolk bare-ass. Anyways, it always comes back to the *dinero.*'

Rocca sighed. 'You got notions of collectin' that bounty, Mack?'

'I got notions of killing 'em all.' McCall gave them all the benefit of his cold gaze. 'But what I really want to collect is my wife, I think Kane took her after burning my ranch.'

'You *think?*'

'Never found a body. No sign of her at all.'

'Well, Kane's known for that kinda thing but how long ago was this? Month? Five weeks. . . ?' Rocca shook his head slowly. 'Sorry, feller, Kane ain't the kind to keep his hostages for long, *never* that long.'

McCall gritted his teeth. 'I can't believe that.'

Rocca's eyes slitted. 'You callin' me a liar?'

'No, I mean, I can't *let* myself believe she's dead. And it's hell if I let myself hope she's still alive.'

That silence again, when no one knew just what to say. 'You're takin' a chance tellin' us,' Rocca pointed out.

'I've got to take chances. It's been too long. I've got to know.'

Rocca pursed his lips. 'Like I already said, I could use a man like you, Mack, or whatever your name is.' He paused but McCall didn't answer. 'Don't matter what you call yourself, I guess, you still got the same job to do.'

'I can't do it alone. Thought I could, but you and your crew could share the bounty, I'm not interested in it.'

Rusty snorted, craning his neck towards the entrance, cupping a gnarled hand behind one ear. 'Any you fellers hear that flappin' sound? Like – mebbe- a pig flyin' by?

The chuckling died fast when they saw McCall's face. He let his gaze rest on Rusty a long moment and the man squirmed a little. McCall turned back to Rocca.

'Why d'you keep him around? He can't cook and he's about as funny as a bunch of piles in a winter line camp.'

Rocca started to lift a placating hand, but it was too late. Rusty had had enough provocation, or had pushed McCall far enough. Rusty came after McCall swinging a dirty skillet. It would have brained the rancher if it had connected, but he ducked under, came up close against the rangy man, left hand groping for the other's right arm. He caught it between wrist and elbow, dug in fingers, finding a nerve he wanted. Rusty showed his mouthful of rotten teeth as he yelled in agony. The skillet fell. McCall stepped back, reached down and grabbed it.

It *bonged* like a distant church bell and Rusty folded in a heap. Denby, the man with the broken nose who

47

had searched McCall's saddle gear stepped in fast, one hand reaching for his sixgun. Another *bong*! and he joined Rusty on the ground, both men moaning sickly.

McCall tossed the skillet aside, backed against the wall, right hand hovering over his gun butt, eyes flicking around the cave, waiting – *ready*.

'Well, if you wanted to gimme a demonstration how good you are, Mack, consider it done,' said Rocca slowly.'But why you so keen to stick with us?'

'I've got an idea where Kane might be, but I don't know this Territory . . . and you fellers live here.'

'How come you know where they might be?'

'I asked a feller.'

'And he told you. . . ?' Rocca asked, disbelievingly.

'Eventually.'

Rocca's eyes narrowed. 'Lemme think about that – "eventually".'

If they were waiting for him to tell them how he had tracked down the scar-faced Mexican member of Kane's bunch for eight days, three of them without sleep, and finally caught up with him at an isolated settler's cabin . . . they'd be waiting a long time. . . .

But just remembering it made him tense, muscles knotted, hands clenching, a few beads of sweat on his brow. . . .

He had picked up the word that Kane's bunch were making a wide south-east swing in their getaway trail. It could only lead to Indian Territory and McCall felt the first risings of panic: once they got in there, surrounded by outlaws and killers, he could lose them forever. And there were signs that some of the gang were breaking away to go it alone, or for some other, unknown reason.

But Kane was the main target to set his sights on.

But what could *he* do? A lone avenger against six or more well-blooded armed killers, and, hopefully, one special hostage. . . ? *Hell! The odds had been the same since he had started after them when Blood's posse gave up. . . .*

'I ain't about to give up!' he'd said aloud and spurred his mount towards a distant smudge that could be a rider's dust. Only a lone rider would make a dust cloud as small as that. . . .

He went after it, a long way off, and the sun going down. By dark, his horse had to rest – and so did he, though he was reluctant to. He looked for a spark in the night that might be a small campfire but saw none. By sun-up he was a mile from his camp and, topping a rise, saw another campsite below, in a narrow arroyo – and a man sprawled near a weathered tent, beside the ashes of a campfire. Both looked to be dead.

But there was a spark of life left in the man, a middle-aged cowman named Sievers, it turned out. A Mexican with a long thin knife scar across the left side of his face had ridden in, all smiles and a sorry story about what he was doing this far north of the Border.Then he had, without warning, tossed the knife he was using to eat the supper Sievers had shared with him into his host's chest.

The Mex finished his meal, then that knife went to work and left Sievers in this bloody, mutilated state. All for thirteen dollars – all the cash Sievers had. The Mexican took his horse and gear, too, left Sievers to bleed to death.

'Said his name was – Chiragua. . . .'

McCall tensed: that was the name of one of Kane's men. Sievers died soon after and McCall took time to bury him then set off after the bloody murderer.

Chiragua knew he was coming, made a pretty good fist of covering his tracks. But not good enough: he couldn't resist temptation, spotted a lonely settler's cabin with female garments on the washing line and simply had to check it out.

There was a man and a woman, both in their fifties, McCall estimated after he had cleaned some of the blood from the bodies. The woman's age hadn't saved her from Chiragua's animal-like abuse. He had hung the man from a tree and used him for target practice. . . .

And was still around – as McCall found out when a rifle cracked from some boulders and the lead spun the hat from his head. Instead of diving for cover, McCall confounded the Mexican by leaping into his saddle and spurring directly for the rocks.

Startled, Chiragua crouched and, in his haste, fumbled the levering of a fresh cartridge into his rifle's breech as McCall leapt the grey over the rock. It landed on top of the Mexican even as he turned to run.

He screamed as the hoofs carved into his back, tore his left ear half off, stomped his belly. McCall dismounted on the run, saw Chiragua, contorted in agony, still trying to reach the big Remington pistol rammed into his belt.

McCall kicked him under the jaw.

When the Mexican came round he found his arms stretched over his head, hands roped to a crooked corral post. His ankles were bound together, too, a rope running from them to McCall's saddle. It was dallied around the horn, and he held the loose end casually.

' 'Bout time you came to.'

'*Señor*! *Señor*! What you do to me. . . ?'

'You can figure it out. Gonna ask you a couple questions. Right after, I'm gonna dig in my spurs – Old Spots here is mighty jumpy, been too long on the trail, needs a good long rest, some oats. But no chance of that for a spell. So, when he feels the touch of my spur rowels. . . .'

'No! *señor*, why you do this to me. . . ?' The wild eyes flew wide as if they would jump right out of the sockets.'Aaaah – *Dios*! It is you! The one Kane thought he killed at that ranch! Ah, but I had nothing to do with that.'

'Shut up – Where's Kane now? And where's my wife?'

The Mexican opened his mouth to say something, a sly look suddenly twisting up his scarred face. But McCall dug in the spurs – and all that came out of Chiragua's mouth was a long, long scream. . . .

It was followed by many others before McCall learned where Kane and his surviving men had gone. *But nothing certain about Rosa*. Chiragua had quit for reasons of his own. She had been alive then, but since, he'd heard Kane had two *black-haired* women with him now. The Mexican was reduced to such abject fear that McCall simply had to believe him.

When Chiragua came round this time, he found his bonds had been removed. He ached terribly, joints strained and twisted, stabbing intolerable pain. Then a rusty spade landed a few inches in front of his face.

He looked up fearfully at McCall towering above him, raised one clasping hand. '*Señor* – I hurt *muy mucho*! Some water – *por favor*. . . .'

'Maybe later . . . after you dig the graves.'

'I cannot dig! I am crippled!'

'You can manage three graves.'

The Mexican frowned, looked sharply at McCall. 'Three. . . ? But. . . .'

'Two for those folk you butchered – then your own.'

CHAPTER 5

A SMALL WAR

'This Chiragua, seems I've heard his name before.' Rocca looked thoughtful. 'Somethin' to do with a killin' south of the Border. One of the Provinces' *gobernadors* as I recollect, or his family. What'd you get outta him?'

'He said Kane was making for a place called Jubilo, I know it means, roughly, jubilation or along those lines, but not where it is, and he didn't say.'

Rocca and his men knew about the place – but maybe not Rusty. He seemed as curious as McCall.

The man with the scarred nose, Denby, said, 'That place above the meadows in The Labrado, ain't it? Injuns used it for pow-wows or somethin', long time ago, lotsa paintin' an' idols. . . .'

Rocca threw the man a cold look. 'Thanks for the information, Denby! Just what Mack wants to know!'

'Well, I thought we was all in it together now.'

Rocca turned to McCall. 'But he's right – Lotsa caves an' paintings and carvings. There're sink holes on the slopes, too, above miles of rolling meadows. . . . You could spot a rattler tryin' to sneak-up on you from up there.'

'Sounds like the kind of place Kane would pick.'

Rocca pursed his lips. 'Good place for defence. But a long ways from anywhere you'd think Kane would go.'

'There's that trail through the Chikashas,' Denby said slowly. 'The one that drops down to the Red River . . . he could make a swing back then, fool everybody.'

Rocca thought about it. 'Why would Kane want to cross *back* into Texas? He's clear now, why go back where he'll be a legitimate target for every lawman or bounty hunter who can walk without crutches?'

'Maybe it was a rendezvous . . . meeting someone there who'd help him escape,' McCall suggested.

Rocca looked dubious. 'Kane knows this place pretty good, but might be somethin' to do with that second woman. Your wife's a hostage, but dunno where the other fits in.'

McCall's eyes were bleak. 'According to the Mex, Kane still has them both with him. Said he'd only met-up with the gang after Jacksboro, he'd been sent to find them, but wouldn't say who sent him. Two women were there then, both with very black hair.' He paused. 'Rosa could've been made to dye hers, I guess.'

Rocca's face was deadpan. 'That's a real wild hope, Mack.'

'I don't have a better one right now. . . . Anyway, what d'you care? You and your men can divvy-up the bounty

– if you can find some way of safely claiming it.'

Rocca smiled thinly. 'You think we don't have a way?'

McCall looked grim. 'I'd hoped the Mex would tell me more, thought I might spook him enough by roughing him up some, then get him to dig his own grave. But he pulled a fast one, tossed a shovelful of gravel at me and came in swinging the spade. I just reacted: shot him twice through the ticker without thinking.'

Rocca pursed his lips. 'Almost as if he knew he was dead anyway, had the last laugh. Forced you to kill him before you made him talk. . . . Wonder why the hell he did that? Don't sound like any Mex I've ever heard of.'

'If I'd been there, he'd've told *everythin'* he knew before I finished him off,' growled Rusty.

McCall glared, wondering at the 'cook' having so much to say in this. 'The thing is, time's running out.'

The outlaw leader gave him a sober look. 'Mack, what you gotta accept is that it might've *already* run out.'

The words slammed McCall like a fist in the teeth. But he knew Rocca was right: he just didn't want to consciously face up to that possibility.

McCall could never have found the place on his own. The trail took them through some of the roughest country he had ever seen – yet they skirted meadows carpeted with clover and sweet-smelling ground-cover with yellow flowers, pine trees trying to poke holes in the scudding clouds, waterfalls, rock faces smooth as glass, others so rough they were like giant sheets of the coarsest sanding-paper.

And that was only leading into the general area.

Resting their mounts at a shaded waterhole, Rocca told him, 'It gets rougher from here on in.'

'How?' McCall sounded bitter, rubbed down the grey's grimy coat with an old shirt.

'Kane knows what he's doin'. We can ride across that big open meadow and either find him gone when we get there – or we don't get there at all. He and his men just pick us off between draws on their cigarettes when we try to climb into the foothills.'

'Why in *hell* would Kane pick a place like this? Why not keep on going? Moving through this area must be slowing him down to hell.'

'Unless he's waitin' for somethin'.' Rusty seemed to be thinking deeply about it: certain signs told McCall that Rusty's true calling was not trail cook: *Anyone who'd eaten one of his meals could testify to that!*

But few men willingly volunteered for cooking chores, so those who did were usually tolerated, even if their efforts weren't the best. There was a limit, of course, but by then the cook was more interested in first aid and remedies for bruises and cuts than flour and beans and coffee you could float a six-shooter in. . . .

McCall pulled himself back with a jolt, wondering why he had allowed himself to be diverted into such ruminating when he might be closer to Rosa than he had been since the Scattergun Gang had pulled their robbery. *The answer was, he was afraid to think too much about her – and what might have happened to her. . . .*

He *had* to hold on to his hope that they had made her dye her hair for some reason and that she was one

56

of the two women travelling with Kane's bunch.

Still travelling with him – he hoped.

'Well, how do we get close enough to Kane to jump him?' The men looked at him sharply. He looked back, spoke coldly. 'One other thing.' His face hardened as he raked them with bleak eyes. 'If my wife's still there, and gets killed in the fracas, she's gonna have company.'

'Now, take it easy,' Rocca told him curtly. 'We'll be careful. But you gotta allow she might be hit by a stray bullet, *No*! You listen, Mack! It could happen. No one's gonna try to shoot the women, but – well, they'll be there so you gotta accept they're at risk. You *gotta*!'

The men were rock-faced, unbending.

McCall's face didn't soften any but there was a slight clouding of his grey eyes: Rocca was right, but it wasn't easy to swallow.

'Let's get started,' he said flatly, taking out his Colt and checking the loads.

'Where the hell did he get so many men!'

It was Rusty who voiced the thoughts of every member of Rocca's gang.

They had come a long, hard trail to get to this position on a ridge that looked down into the Scattergun Gang's camp in a small hollow below. Jubilo. . . .

They expected to find, at the most, six or seven men and, hopefully, as far as McCall was concerned, the two women. There was at least a dozen down there, and he saw a small lean-to at one side, near a narrow cutting that overlooked the big meadow which they had avoided.

A rope had been strung to the low branch of a small tree close by and several feminine garments and under-garments were hanging from it.

At least one of the women was still alive! Not normally religious, he added, *Lord, please let it be Rosa!*

But Kane had all those men with him now. One was another Mexican and there was a man dressed like a riverboat gambler. Or, maybe he was what McCall thought of as a so-called 'Louisiana gentleman', like one he'd once seen: *one of those arrogant, swaggering 'gentlemen' who frequented smoky, dream-filled opium dens in New Orleans, or high-stakes gambling camps hidden in the bayous and backwater swamps. . . .*

What a man like that would be doing here with the likes of Kane and his murderous crew was something McCall couldn't work out.

Crouching by a rock on the ledge above the camp, he gave it one more careful inspection then concentrated on that lean-to, willing the women to appear in the low doorway.

Or just one! The right one. . . .

'We can't wait any longer.' Rocca gestured to the sun's disc starting to slide towards the distant ranges. 'They'll put up a fight and they'll hold out till dark then make a run for it . . . and take our bounty with 'em!'

'Yeah, let's get it done!' growled Rusty and his rifle came up and whip-cracked in four hammering shots: there was no choice now – *they had to attack.*

Below, dust spurted beside a man sitting sewing a cinch ring more securely into a belly-strap, a man's coffee mug spun into the air, trailing dark liquid, and

58

another man clasped at his upper arm, staggered side-ways – into the path of the fourth bullet. He was flung on to his back at the edge of the campfire. By that time, the Scattergun gang, long experienced at being on the wrong end of a manhunt, living on a knife-edge of tension and stress every minute, had thrown the contents of the coffee pot over the fire and men were on the run. They scattered in all directions, didn't bunch-up, so making easy shooting for whoever was up on the rim: they dispersed widely, knowing whoever was up there was going to have to spread his gunfire to find a target.

It was every man for himself.

Still, Kane's men knew their positions for defence. Two men, running, snatched weapons from a stand of rifles stacked army-fashion, easy to reach. The rest of the stack clattered in collapse but there were ready hands waiting to grab a weapon even as it fell.

The outlaws rolled and crouched, spinning over small mounds of earth and gravel, lying prone behind rocks, immediately finding the source of the attack. Levers worked and muzzles spat fire, bright as a ragged line of berserk fireflies in the gathering dusk, bullets raking the attackers' cover.

One of Rocca's men screamed briefly as a slug took him in the throat: he was rising up from the prone posi-tion at the time, and the lead tore down through vital organs all the way to his belly. The blood-curdling sound of his dying briefly stopped the shooting. Then someone cursed a blue streak and guns opened up in a volley that raked the attackers' ridge fiercely, forcing them to hunch down, slide back below the mounds of their earthworks. A storm of stones and dirt clods scattered over their heads and writhing bodies.

'Judas priest!' someone grated. 'You sure this ain't the Little Big Horn!'

Then a rifle cracked from behind and above them – it had to be the guard they had avoided when making their way in here. His bullets killed another of Rocca's men, shattering the luckless outlaw's spine.

The convulsing man had been right beside McCall. He spun on to his back, levering, smoking muzzle tracking swiftly and picking out the guard on the ledge above. The man was down on one knee, sighting-in on Rusty. McCall yelled a warning, then they fired together, McCall and the guard. Rusty spun violently, sliding over the ridge for several feet. The guard rose slightly, McCall's first shot having missed, beading Rusty for the killing shot. McCall straightened, taking a chance, and triggered two fast shots. He threw himself sideways, across the man whose spine had been smashed. The bullet from above *thunked* into the dead man and McCall's lever blurred, jacking in the next cartridge, the trigger squeezing instantly. The guard reared up, rifle toppling over the ledge as he clawed at his bloody face with both hands.

He fell forward off the ledge but McCall didn't watch, spun towards the main defence line where guns were roaring continuously: it could well have been taken for a pitched battle between opposing sides in The War that had ended almost twenty years ago.

Three outlaws were sprawled down below, two lying

still, one man trying to crawl away into some rocks. Denby stood up, like a jack-in-the-box being released, triggered and dropped down again before anyone below could draw a bead on him. Rusty lay very still at the foot of the small slope, blood on his side and one leg.

McCall reloaded his hot rifle, cursing the pall of gunsmoke that now blurred the camp below. He couldn't make out the lean-to clearly but thought there were riders close to it. The scattering men below took advantage of the powdersmoke fog, running to the edge of the camp and leaping over into what was probably an arroyo. Then, through the rattle of gunfire, throwing his rifle to his shoulder, McCall heard the whinny of horses, the clatter of hoofs.

'They've got to their broncs!' he yelled, standing recklessly, trying to see over the edge of the arroyo. He glimpsed a man's hat, fired, but it disappeared behind a rock. Another rider showed briefly and Rocca blew him out of the saddle with two speedy shots. There was a thunder of scatterguns below now, too – they made a flatter, louder *crrraaaack* than the bellowing boom of a normal shotgun.

One of Rocca's men screamed and tumbled, both hands pressing into his shot-torn belly. McCall dropped low in an effort to see below that damn smoke.

Then someone screamed: 'Dynamite!'

He clawed at the ground, saw the dark oblongs of two bundles of dynamite sticks with sputtering fuses sailing through the air towards the slope. As he ducked they fell and exploded with an ear-shattering sound that briefly disoriented him. Dust and stones and clods of earth rained down. There were bodies lying around, but some were merely stunned by the blast, sat up groggily – and that cursed dust cloud gave mighty good cover to the escaping outlaws. . . .

McCall slid and toppled and rolled down the slope. Rocca's few remaining men skidded after him so that he had their dust to contend with as well as the gunsmoke and the pall raised by the dynamite.

Coughing and spitting, he surged out of the haze, blinking, saw a shadowy shape lifting a gun in his direction and fired the rifle with the butt against his hip. The muzzle rode up and the bullet *splatted* as it hit the man in the face and lifted him clear of the ground, hurling him over a yard. He fell, unmoving. Then, running on towards the lean-to McCall saw with a cold surge of goosebumps all over his sweating body that it had been partly wrecked by the dynamite's blast. One corner sagged drunkenly and the clothes line lay in the dust, garments trampled. The ground in front was torn up by the hoofs of at least three horses.

He ripped off sheets of the bark that had been used to roof the structure. His attention was diverted to trees below where several riders were making their escape, but he didn't see Kane – or any women – among them. The 'gambler' was there, though, mounted and surrounded by the others: as if being protected. . . .

Panting, kicking wildly, McCall splintered supporting saplings, dropped his rifle and heaved mightily, hurling most of the lean-to's roof to one side. Sweat streaming down his face, he blinked, wiped the back of a hand across his stinging eyes – and felt his heart skip a beat.

There were no bodies. Only several splotches of fresh blood on the hard packed earthen floor.

Lying in one, its dark green-and-white border now coloured red, was a neckerchief he had given Rosa for her last birthday, with a matching head scarf.

CHAPTER 6

THE PREACHER'S

Rocca was in a foul mood: his band had been decimated. No one had figured on Kane and his gang meeting with more men, men who could put up a hard fight, too.

'Judas priest!' Rocca lamented when they stood at the edge of the arroyo where the Scattergun Gang and their allies had kept the getaway mounts. 'We're down to four men! And Rusty's wounded, no damn good for pursuit.'

'He needs a sawbones,' opined McCall and earned himself a baleful stare from Rocca.

'I'll pay for one for him, after I get that bounty!'

Denby, nursing a right arm that had been gouged by buckshot, snapped his head up. 'Hey, Rock! I could do with some doctorin', too! I got half a pound of buckshot in me.'

'I'll dig 'em out for you,' volunteered Rocca with a

twisted smile, and then dropped a hand to his gunbutt as a dust-covered man came lurching up, breathless. 'Where the hell you been, Lefty? I counted you as among the dead.'

'I fell down with Kane's men and played possum till I was sure he'd gone. Was lyin' right next a feller who was dyin'.' Lefty had a wall-eye and it rolled around to fix McCall with as steady a stare as the man could manage, though Lefty still spoke to Rocca. 'Turned out he was Jared Parkes' kid brother. You recall Jared, Rock? Rode with us on that swing station deal south of Amarillo. . . ?'

'I remember Parkes,' Rocca growled. 'Tried to snitch the damn strong box while we were holdin' back the posse. . . .'

'Yeah – well, *this* Parkes told me the bounty on Kane's gang ain't anythin' like what this feller says.'

All eyes turned to McCall and, still staring at the rancher, Rocca said, 'That so. . . ? What did Parkes say. . . ?'

Lefty's reddened eyes narrowed. 'He reckons it's no more'n ten thousand, thinks mebbe nine-an'-some-thin'.'

Rocca, face flat and hard, nodded slowly, gaze deadly as it held on McCall's grim features. 'Just a little short of what you told us, Mack.'

'Eighteen thousand was what I heard.'

'Then you heard wrong! You pulled a figure outta the air, I reckon. So we'd help you run down Kane – so *you* could find your wife!'

McCall nodded slowly. 'Yeah, OK. I needed someone

who knew this country to back me. I lied about the bounty to get you interested. But ten grand's not bad, 'specially now there's only the four of you left to share.'

Lefty spat, jumping upright, hand sweeping towards his gun butt. 'You lousy. . . .'

He brought his gun up and McCall threw himself to one side, drawing and shooting while moving. Lefty was slammed over backwards, his Colt firing into the ground.

'Watch out!' someone yelled.

McCall spun to the left already diving for the ground as Denby, slightly behind, triggered. The lead passed over McCall's falling body and then, elbows planted in the dirt, his Colt bucked and roared twice. Denby sat down, looking surprised and opened his mouth as if to speak – blood poured out instead of words and he toppled sideways.

'*Rocca!*' This time McCall recognized the warning voice as Rusty's: the words were raspy, gasped out with a lot of effort.

On one knee, McCall swung back, wrenching his head aside as Rocca's bullet whipped past his face. He triggered a single shot and Rocca was hurled back. The bullet, slanting upwards, lifted him to his toes, before his legs gave way and he collapsed, curling on to his left side, almost as if he were asleep – but it was a sleep from which he would never awaken.

McCall stood, smoking pistol cocked and ready for more trouble, but there was no more: couldn't be any more.

Apart from Rusty, Rocca's gang was wiped out.

Reloading, McCall stood over Rusty. 'Twice you saved my neck just then. Why?'

Rusty's ugly face was blotched red-and-grey and although tight with pain, his eyes twinkled just a little.

'Figured . . . you'd be the one to . . . get me to a . . . sawbones.'

McCall paused in his reloading. 'Out here?'

Rusty nodded, obviously in a good deal of pain from his wounds. 'The Preacher's. . . .'

'What the hell's "The Preacher's"?'

'A kinda tradin' post run by an ex-preacher an' his wife. She's a Negress, sings Gospel hymns over the wounded and sick while the Preacher works on 'em.'

McCall looked at him dubiously but it was obvious Rusty was in no mood for frivolity.

'And what makes you think I'll take you there?'

Just for a moment, there was a flash of uncertainty in Rusty's eyes and then his thin-lipped mouth twisted into a smile.

'Because you're basically decent, Mack . . . an' I don't reckon that's your name. Even doubt if you're really on the run.' McCall said nothing and, sweating with the effort of talking, Rusty added, 'You can claim the bounty on Rocca, help you in your search for your wife.'

McCall frowned: *that made sense, though of course, he had hoped that he would catch up with Kane quickly and find Rosa alive, and . . . and maybe even unharmed. . . .*

Even as the thoughts swirled through his aching brain, he knew he was being over-optimistic, still. . . .

'You were lying on the ledge, just above where they

had the getaway mounts. Did you see the women with Kane when he lit-out?'

Rusty took his time before he shook his head slowly. McCall's mouth tightened into a razor-thin line.

Well, he could also use the bounty to hunt down Kane if Rosa was already dead. An unwanted alternative, but there.

The Negress had an easy-to-listen-to contralto voice that trembled on some of the notes, adding emphasis and passion to her words, though the hymn she had chosen for Rusty wouldn't have given him much comfort, McCall thought – '*Swing Low, Sweet Chariot – Comin' For To Carry Me Home. . . .*'

As the Preacher, a nuggety, hard-muscled man who looked more like a railroad gandy-dancer than a medico, deftly stitched the large wound in Rusty's chest – the exit wound from his back – the man's eyes fluttered half-open.

'Doc,' he said in a hoarse whisper. 'Tell that, that damn angel to quit singin'. I, I ain't goin' nowhere, in a chariot, stagecoach nor nothin' else.'

His words slurred away and the Preacher looked up. A small smile crossed his gnarled face. 'Most of them say the same thing, use almost the exact same words. But Peach Blossom knows that hymn scares 'em silly and many a man who was ready to give up the fight rallies – just to spite her.' He chuckled. 'Lovely voice, though, isn't it?'

McCall nodded. 'You tend other folk who stop by?'

'We tend *anybody* who stops by, young feller. Everyone is welcome in our house, everyone. We're all

The Lord's children.'

McCall was wary of a possible, forthcoming religious lecture and said quickly, 'By the way, I noticed Rusty had a lot of blood on his left leg, too, Doc, showing on the high legging part of his moccasins. Think he must've gashed it when he fell over the ledge.'

'Yes, I noticed that myself but his chest wound was the more serious. Care to take a look at the leg while I finish here?'

McCall struggled to get the shoe part of the soft buckskin legging over the heel and then it slid down more easily. Rusty rolled his head and moaned in sudden pain. McCall looked sharply at the medic, stopping his tugging.

'Seems to be something caught inside the legging. Hell, it's cut a gash halfway down his calf. Not deep, but—'

The Preacher leaned closer, frowned, took the moccasin from McCall, feeling the soft legging part with his blunt fingers. 'Something here all right, sharp like a needle. Why, there's a little pocket. . . . Hardly noticeable, just a slit for entry.' He probed while talking. 'Hullo – what on earth. . . ?' He fumbled with the bloodstained section and something popped out, made a dull metallic ring as it fell to the floor.

Even Peach Blossom stopped singing as all three stared at the item as it slowly stopped spinning.

It was a badge, a star within a circle that was engraved – *US MARSHAL.*

'Used to have it pinned to my underwear but the damn

pin kept springin' out and stabbin' me at the most awkward times. So I made that pocket in the leggin' to hold it.'

Rusty was propped half upright on pillows in the narrow bed in the Preacher's back room, his chest and leg bandaged now. He looked gaunt and drawn with the pain, greyish face sheened with sweat, but managed a brief smile as he studied McCall.

'Told you I knew a marshal carried his badge in his underwear. Just forgot to mention it was me.'

'Why carry a badge at all if you're working undercover like that? I mean, if Rocca or someone had seen it. . . .'

'You'd be surprised how many doors that badge can open. It's worth the risk, *necessary* to have some identification at times. If you take a man into court and haven't shown him your authority when you first arrest him, like your badge, some snake-smart lawyer'll get him off on the technicality. There's a number on the back, too. All another lawman has to do is look it up in a special book they have and I can get all the co-operation I need.'

McCall smiled wryly. 'I thought you were trying to make Rocca think I might be the undercover marshal.'

'I was,' Rusty admitted easily. 'Figured it might take any suspicions off me,' Rusty said. 'I think he was gettin' leery about me, and you had the look of a hardcase so I prodded you into goin' for your gun—' He stopped and sobered slowly. 'I tell you, just for a moment there, when you brought that Colt out so fast I couldn't see nothin' but the light flashin' from the barrel – well, I thought I'd gone too far and you were gonna blast me.'

'Came close, you don't have the sweetest disposition, Rusty.'

'I was just gettin' into my role as a cook: they're always crusty, for some reason,' Rusty cackled. 'Act the mean ol' bastard pretty well, don't I? Used it as a cover for so long I am a mean of bastard now – and me a gran'pappy!'

'Pity your grandkids.'

'Aaah – you wouldn't know me back in my parlour in San Antone, sittin' on the floor with my toes pokin' outta a pair of old felt slippers, playin' with my gran'-daughter and grandson. . . .'

His eyes took on a dreamy look and, although McCall found it hard to imagine, he kept silent, as Rusty thought back to his other life. Then he sighed and reluctantly returned to the present.

'Meant it about Rocca's bounty bein' able to help you track down Kane, Mack – What is your name, by the way?' McCall told him and Rusty nodded briefly. 'I ain't gonna be able to ride for some time accordin' to the Preacher . . . I said I never seen any women with Kane's bunch as they escaped. I was lookin' more at that river-boat gambler type the way they seemed to be nursin' him along. But there was two riders out front with one of Kane's men, and they were wearin' ponchos. Only seen 'em from the back: they weren't very tall in the saddle, an' their hats were small—'

'Two of them?' McCall asked tautly, holding his breath.

Rusty nodded. 'Yeah – about the size of two women, I'd say.'

71

McCall *wanted* to believe him, but Rusty Searles – his real name he claimed – had an easy-sounding tongue that could smoothly slip into downright lies without a hiccup.

'You wouldn't just be saying this – because you want me to go after Kane while you're laid-up, would you?'

It was amazing how quickly and easily Rusty's battered face could take on an offended innocence: maybe the genuine pain he was feeling slowed him down a mite, but not much. He really looked hurt at McCall's suggestion.

'Well, you might've said it in a better *tone*, but—' He cleared his throat and nodded slowly. 'OK – I admit I been thinking you'd be a good man to go after Kane, all right – someone I could trust.'

'Why would you think that, on our short acquaintance?'

Rusty smiled crookedly. 'You saved my life, didn't you? By the by, you wear insoles in your ridin' boots?'

McCall, caught off-guard, felt his jaw sag slightly and then he frowned. 'Funny question!'

'Just wondered. Lotsa fellers do, if their feet give 'em trouble – an' what cowboy's feet don't? Or, if they want to hide somethin': something small and flat, like a paper wrapped in onionskin to protect it.'

The Preacher was frowning, too, but at McCall and the stunned expression on the man's face. 'Are you all right, Mr McCall. . . ?'

'No, not really.' He gestured to the chuckling Rusty who suddenly stopped as pain shot through his chest wound and he grabbed at the bandage. The Preacher was leaning over him in a moment, rearranging the pillows, telling Rusty to try not to cough too hard.

'Would you tell my wife I'll need her help for a few minutes. . . ? You can come in after we've made some adjustments to the wound and its bandages. . . .'

McCall hesitated, reluctant to leave right now, but went and fetched Peach Blossom and had a smoke on the weathered porch of the old trading post. He had finished the cigarette before the woman told him he could go back and see Rusty now.

'What is going on between you two?' The Preacher asked as soon as he entered, Rusty looking a little brighter, but still obviously in a lot of pain. There was a smear or two of fresh blood on the new bandage over the chest wound.

'Rusty's question – a strange one I admit! – about your boots seemed to upset you, while he looked like the cat that had swallowed the canary.'

McCall sighed. 'I'm on friendly terms with Major Usher at Fort Garnett. He gave me a written authority to arrest Kane if I was able to find him and any members of his gang. It probably doesn't hold water but it acts like an approval from the army, sort of telling folk I'm trustworthy, I guess.' He flicked his eyes to Rusty who had settled down now. 'How he knows I hid that paper in my boot lining, or even how it exists, beats the hell outta me.'

Rusty lifted a hand. 'Happened I was in Fort Garnett not long after you left. I'm a friend of the major's, too, and he mentioned you could be trusted and if we met up in the Territory, we might help each other. . . .'

'Well, it was a long shot, but I guess it paid off seeing as we were both working the same area – but what're you getting at now? About that paper?'

'Just confirmin' I have the right man. Bein' a federal lawman, I can give you authority to collect the bounty on Rocca. Then I'll give you a name and you can use some of that money to buy information about Kane – I won't kid you: it'll cost plenty, and Vern's a treacherous bastard, but I know you want Kane almost as bad as I do. . . .'

'Worse.'

Rusty paused, nodded curtly. 'Yeah. These women and that riverboat gambler feller, they worry me. I figure they weren't in Kane's original getaway plans, but he's been careful so far as we know with the women – and now this gambler feller's joined him and it looks very much like Kane and what's left of his gang are actin' like guards. Protectin' him, *takin' him somewhere.*'

'That's the impression I got, too,' spoke up the Preacher suddenly.

McCall frowned. 'Kane was here?'

'He had wounded, too – and as I told you, all are welcome.'

'Preacher told me about it just now while he was fixin' my wound, McCall. The Frenchy stopped one low in his back, but it'll only slow him down a little. . . .' At McCall's puzzled look, he added, 'The gambler – he's French.'

'D'you know who he is?'

'I dunno as I want to say just yet. You gonna do what I ask? Collect that bounty and buy the information,

74

then act on it?'

'Provided it'll help me get Rosa back.'

'Aw, listen, I can't guarantee she's still alive! But even if she isn't – and if I'm thinkin' right – I'd want you to follow-through.'

'I can't give you *my* word on that.'

Rusty swore and was silent for a time, then asked the Preacher to leave the room for a few minutes. The man complied without question and after the door had closed, Rusty gestured for McCall to come closer. He spoke in a low voice.

'Would you do it if I said I thought that gambler-type was the one tried to shoot the President? And Kane was helpin' him get away? Huh? What d'you say to that?'

CHAPTER 7

THE POOR ONES

The Frenchman's instructions were quite clear: *leave no witnesses.*

The raid must be made to look as if it was carried out by Indians – no one must find even a hint that it was done by Kane's band of killers.

'After all, this place is known as "Indian Territory" or "The Cherokee Strip",' the Frenchman – Jacques L'Vende – said in his accented English. When he spoke he held his head tilted slightly, his long face haughty, the pencil moustache fringing his thin upper lip twitching slightly. 'Why should they not take the, er, credit, eh?'

Scattergun Kane and his men had no thoughts one way or another: they would do what they were being paid for. No more, and no less.

The Frenchman cared nothing about Los Pobres and its work with the poor and ailing: to him, it was merely another step along the trail to where he wished to go. *And one about which he had unpleasant memories – but not after today. . . .*

'Fortunately, the Mission is isolated – another sign of our good luck, no?'

If he had hoped for some response from Kane and his men he was disappointed, though he did not register it. Perhaps the black eyes pinched down a little, possibly.

'There you will find the so-called *Fathers* and the *Sisters of Mercy*. I do not know how many but that hardly matters. You will have no trouble with them. In any case, they will be far outnumbered by the poor they are offering succour. Once again, *leave no witnesses*. Get everything on the list I have given you, then, within reason, help yourself to whatever else takes your fancy, as long as it can not be traced back to Los Pobres!'

'We know what to do. Might be a good idea to burn the place afterwards.' Kane was a man who enjoyed the spectacle of burning buildings. He bit into a hot biscuit one of the dark-haired women had baked. 'Injuns like burnin' what they wreck. . . . It's like a trademark.'

'I agree, and there is also one more unmistakable trade-mark of an Indian attack.'

'Yeah? What?' Kane did not take to this French dandy, smelling of lavender, and who spoke to him as if he were a five year old kid. But he paid well, that was what mattered.

L'Vende arched his eyebrows, touched a thumbnail to his hairline, paused, then whipped it across the dark, pomaded curls, making a vague hissing sound.

'Aw, you mean scalps? No trouble. Just make sure the second payment is ready.' Kane glared coldly, not adding *Or else!* His words were met with a look that was bleak and disdainful. Shrugging, he hipped around and called, 'Cookie. Bring me more biscuits. You bake pretty good, for frontier trash.'

The small dark-haired woman in the torn poncho, crouching by the camp fire, placed two more golden biscuits on a platter. A second woman sat with her back to a rock, also wearing an old poncho, but with hers pushed back over wide shoulders, revealing a blood-smeared bandage on her upper left arm. She watched with hooded, dark eyes, squarish face expressionless, as she smoked a cheroot. Smoke streamed in twin plumes from pinched nostrils and between thin-lips.

'Cookie', eyes lowered, chin tucked in, reached out to pass the platter to Kane. He took it, then, with his other hand grabbed her slim wrist, tugging her almost off-balance.

'Hey – don't go 'way. Sit here beside me. C'mon, Cookie, you want me to take off my belt and lay into you again? Mebbe you liked that, uh?'

She cringed involuntarily, pulled back a little, but, watching his face, slowly sat down beside him, leaving a couple of feet of space between them.

'My name is not "Cookie",' she told him curtly, in a voice that carried a wary tremor. She was as tense as a crouching cougar cub, waiting for an eagle with ready talons to descend upon it.

Kane laughed, looked around at the other men, ignoring the stiff-faced Frenchman and the second woman. 'Hey, fellers, think I'm startin' to get through here! Couple of weeks ago she'd have kicked me and tried to scratch my eyes out!'

'Must be your fatal charm, boss,' one man chuckled.

'That it, Cookie? You think I'm charmin'?' He tried to chuck her under the chin but she jerked her head aside, curling a lip.

'I think you stink worse than a pig!'

Kane's face straightened and he set down the platter wiping his fingers on his grimy shirt. Silently, he began to unbuckle his wide trouser belt. Fearful now, she whirled and tried to run away. But he tripped her, got to his knees and, as she sprawled, feet straddling her, laid the belt across her shoulders. She cried out in pain and rolled on to her side, face ivory-white, dark eyes wide, contrasting with her pallor as she tried to protect her head.

As she did so, a few strands of reddish-gold hair spilled out from beneath the head scarf she wore, dirty white with a green border, to help keep the black wig in place.

'Pity you won't be with us for much longer, Cookie,' Kane said, teeth bared as he took a deep breath. 'I'm gonna miss you. But, till then you – *do – like – I – say*!'

She raised her hands protectively as the belt whistled towards her again – and again – and again. . . .

The name Rusty had given McCall was Vernon Kettle.

'He's a come-day, go-day, turnin' a dollar any way he can: he'll do anythin' for a buck, and I mean *anythin'* – yeah, he's on a few Wanted dodgers but he's useful to us at times, so the Marshals and the Rangers turn a blind eye.'

McCall nodded at Rusty Searles where he sat amidst his throne-like pillows in the Preacher's infirmary. 'Where'll I find him?'

Rusty, lined face sagging with the pain he had already endured and was still suffering, smiled thinly. 'His place is just inside the Territory, t'other side of the Red River, almost nudging Texas. He hears Marshals or a posse're headin' his way, he slips deeper into the Strip. He knows they can't hassle him without a Federal warrant.'

'Sounds smart.'

'Cunnin' as a fox stalkin' a chicken coop. Bein' where he is, he runs a kind of "underground railway" into the Territory for those who need it – and who can pay. He stays in our good books by lettin' us know the movements back and forth across the line.'

McCall nodded as he rolled a cigarette and put it between Rusty's thin, purplish lips. He thumbed a match into flame and lit the smoke, then his own, already dangling from his lips. 'Trustworthy as a sick rattler.'

'Mebbe, but he gets all the news without havin' to even leave his place – he'll pass along somethin' useful to us when it suits him: point is, it suits us and the fellers on the run can't afford to be fussy, have to hope he'll see 'em right.'

'Wonder he's still breathing.'

'Hell, yeah. But there's always a price an' Ol' Vernon's greedy enough to take the risk.'

'You think he'll know about Kane? And Rosa. . . ?'

Rusty took the cigarette from his mouth with a shaky hand and exhaled, rheumy eyes on McCall's anxious face. 'If anybody can tell you, it'll be Vern Kettle.'

'He can have the whole damn Rocca bounty if he wants. Long as he gives me what *I* want.'

Rusty nodded slowly. 'I b'lieve that, McCall – and I wish you luck. I'll give you an authorization for you to claim the bounty but you'll have to go to Wichita Falls.'

'That's a helluva way!'

'It is – but the sheriff there is my brother-in-law. He'll speed things up. Listen, you do like I say and it'll go smoother all round. Get that bounty, even if you have to wait-over a couple days. It'll buy you what you want to know. Before you know it, you'll have Kane in your sights.'

'I'll want to talk with that son of a bitch before I pull the trigger.'

Rusty smiled faintly. 'I b'lieve that, too!'

He was champing at the bit now. It had taken three days for just part of the bounty to come through. Two thousand dollars of the five posted. Rusty's brother-in-law Lance Collie, had done his best and now McCall was spurring the dappled grey out of the muddy Red River, searching for the broken, lopsided peak Rusty had told him to look for.

Vernon Kettle's place was a couple of miles southeast of that peak, hidden way back in a serpentine canyon. McCall felt some of the tension drain from him when he finally located the odd-shaped peak. He

81

glanced at the sun, south of his present position, and saw another landmark Rusty had mentioned, a red butte, on the Texas side of the river.

Riding with the broken peak and that butte in line would take him to Vern Kettle's place. He used the spurs sparingly on the weary grey. *With any luck, he ought to be there by sundown. . . .*

He was, but he almost didn't make it.

Rusty had warned him how careful Vern Kettle was but he hadn't said anything about the man being willing to shoot trespassers without warning. McCall should have figured it for himself: a man riding the knife edge of treachery and greed like Kettle would need to take all kinds of pre-cautions: men he sent into the waiting arms of the Law were going to be released from jail some day . . . and remember who put them there.

The rifle shot banged and bounced off the broken rocks of the twisting narrow canyon and the bullet all but singed his left ear before ricocheting three, *four*, times.

By then McCall was out of the saddle, slapping the spooked grey on the rump with his hat, his other hand palming up his Colt. He dropped behind a rock as the horse ran out of sight.

'Now ain't you the foolish one!' a voice called from somewhere amongst the rocks. 'Lettin' that good ol' geldin' run off like that. Why it's not thirty yards from me and I've got a bead on his head that'll drop him like a rock down a well. . . . Unless you'd kinda like to stand up – slow, very slow . . . hands empty.'

McCall swore under his breath but didn't move.

'I ain't the most patient of men, mister. I meant to miss your ear, so don't think that was lousy shootin' – I'll give you a five-count, a *quick* one, an' if you don't. . . .'

'All right, Kettle! Rusty Searles sent me.'

Taking a chance, McCall straightened slowly, holding the Colt by two fingers. He saw sunlight flash from a rifle barrel on the rim, not twenty yards away: he would make an easy target standing here like this . . . sweat trickled down inside his shirt.

'Good ol' Rusty, huh? Well, we done business before. I know him well enough he wouldn't send you along unless you're able to pay your way.'

McCall grinned. 'Yeah, he said you were kinda mercenary.'

'Only way to live. OK, leather that Colt and come ahead slow. I can get your hoss – or you – in less than a second if I have to an' I'm the one decides.'

McCall obeyed and followed further directions, walking around some rocks and into a deep bend where the grey stood, ears pricked, eyes showing white, poised to run. But it stayed put when it recognized McCall, whinnied softly in greeting.

A shadow moved across the ground in front of McCall and he lifted his eyes to see a man rising from behind a boulder, a carbine held deceptively casually. He was an average-size man, maybe early forties – that surprised McCall: Rusty had referred to Kettle several times as *Old* Vern. He wore a dark brown, pinstriped suit, trousers, jacket and vest. A somewhat battered

Derby hat sat canted to the left on his head. *Dressed for a funeral, mebbe?*

Not his, McCall hoped!

At the man's request McCall gave his name and when he did he thought the dust-reddened eyes narrowed just a fraction. 'You won't find me on any dodgers.'

'Mebbe not, but I've heard talk of you recently.'

'Rusty said you were pretty smart, the "smart" part I believe.'

Kettle laughed. 'Sassy son of a bitch! I could shoot your eye out from here.'

'Let's talk first – I may make you rich.'

'You better at least add to my stash or we won't do no deal.'

'Like I said, let' s talk.'

Vern Kettle had a well-built split-log cabin with a shingle roof, standing almost against one of the canyon's walls. He had obviously made the furniture himself from available timber growing close to hand, in such a way that the cabin was hidden – unless a man got so far into that part of the canyon that he cleared the trees. *Dangerous! Unless Kettle wanted it that way. He was king here. . . .*

Carbine close to his hand all the time, Kettle brewed coffee and cut up some cold venison and goat's cheese while McCall told him his story. As he sat down at the solid table and they began to eat, he said, casually,

'There was $5,000 bounty on Rocca, I believe.' McCall brought in a small package from his saddle-bags and slapped it down in front of Kettle.

'Two thousand. All that came through. Some damn

rigamarole with the rest, Sheriff Collie in Wichita Falls wrote a note to that effect to show I'm not fibbin'. I couldn't wait. Figured you'd be willing to take a down-payment.'

'That's all this is, make a damn good note of that!' Kettle shook the stack of notes and put them into a vest pocket. 'Guess you're anxious about your wife, huh? She's one of the women with Kane?'

'Was hoping you could tell me for sure.'

'Never heard no names and they kept the women under close guard. Can't swear she's still alive now, even – Kane came through about a week ago. Apart from his killers and the women, he's got a mighty nasty feller ridin' with him.'

'That Frenchman?'

Kettle nodded, showing mild surprise.

'So you know about him?' He took off the old Derby hat and began brushing it with the rather loose sleeve of his suit jacket. His hair was short and grey-specked. 'Calls himself L'Vende – likes lavender, as you might see by his clothes: and I been told he sprinkles a little on himself at times. Not important. Ladies' man, too, I hear, but his main claim to fame is he's a duellist.'

'A what?'

'Gamblin' man who hardly ever loses, mostly because he accuses the player beatin' him of cheatin'. Takes an insult or a slap in the puss for it, but that gives him the right to challenge the man to a duel. He's never lost one yet, killed every man who was stupid enough to go up agin him. Shot 'em all right between the eyes.'

'A dead shot. And not just with a duelling pistol,

85

Rusty tells me.'

Kettle's bushy eyebrows arched. 'You hear he be the one took that shot at the President, eh?'

'Rusty thinks he's the man.'

'Lot of folk do, but I dunno, it ain't his style, though I've heard he can knock the eye out of a turkey at a hundred yards – and come to think of it, there's a rumour about some big trouble brewin' over some kinda Louisiana land deal he was mixed-up in. Coupla families died in fires that burned 'em out – and one of 'em had mighty powerful kin in the East – L'Vende'd risk just about anythin' if it pays well enough and there's all the sign that Kane's helpin' him get to Mexico. He's here in the Territory for some reason, whether it's dodgin' the land deal or tryin' to shoot the President. Whatever it is, it's gotta be important or payin' almighty good.'

McCall moved impatiently. 'Let's skip the Frenchman. It's my wife I'm interested in.'

Kettle rose, went to a well-made cupboard with dove-tailed joints and took out a folded map. He spread it on the table. 'Here's my place – and – here—' He moved a finger across to a point deep in the Territory. 'Here's where I think Kane is headed. If he keeps goin' he'll hit the Prairie-Dog Fork of the Red eventually and. . . .'

'That's a helluva way! He wouldn't need to go that far, would he? I mean once he's well past the Texas line, he's got all the cover he needs in the Territory – not many lawmen would follow that far. They could be cut off too easy.'

Kettle looked at him calculatingly. McCall frowned,

sensing he was about to hear something he didn't want to.

'Kane goes that far, and after a short trip down-river, it's only a frog's leap to the Mississippi and Baton Rouge. . . .'

'The hell're we talking about the Mississippi for. . . ? That's a couple of hundred miles away, for Chris'sakes!'

'Don't take long to get there by riverboat, and they run all the way to New Orleans . . . where it's easy to pick up a schooner and sail across the Gulf to Vera Cruz.'

McCall's hands clenched. He felt the knotting of his belly, staring dully at Kettle. 'By God! Looks like that Frenchy did take the potshot at the President! He's running scared, got plenty of protection with Kane, who's also on the run and pretty damn desperate. Likely got all kinds of escape routes set up in Mexico.'

'McCall—? You're right – but you gotta realize Kane's usin' the White Slavers' trail. He'll be safe down in Mexico. So'll the Frenchman—' He paused. 'The Mexes'll go loco over the women, specially that wife of yours, she being a *rubio*: that red-gold hair drives 'em plumb loco I hear. An' if it's natural, and she's got it . . . another place as well, there'll be plenty of blood flowin' when them greasers fight each other to get to her.'

McCall hit him. A short sharp blow, knuckles slamming against the man's jaw. Kettle staggered back, dragged a chair with him as he sat down heavily. He blinked, ran a tongue around inside his lips, tasting blood.

'No call for that, you bastard!'

'Nor for you slobbering over what can happen to Rosa!' McCall gritted, nostrils flaring, chest heaving, fists still clenched. Kettle got slowly and warily to his feet.

'Face up to it, McCall! Kane's gettin' outta the US and usin' your wife to finance himself for a better life in good ol' *manana* land. It might be a bitter pill for you to swallow, but it's gonna happen, whether you like it or not. . . . First it'll be the rich *rancheros*, then, after a while, she'll be shuffled into a brothel, an'. . . .'

'Shut up, Kettle!' It hurt like hell, but McCall was forced to admit: Kettle was right.

Rosa, with her beautiful hair, the kind which the Mexicans particularly worshipped, was on her way to becoming a slave in a brothel, where she would no doubt be drugged and degraded until—

Massaging his swelling jaw, Kettle slurred, smiling nastily. 'One other thing, McCall, you're never gonna catch up with Kane before he gets to Vera Cruz. You've lost too much ground. Your wife's gone now – forever!'

'You son of a bitch! You just had to rub it in, didn't you!'

'Wanted to make sure you died in the right frame of mind!'

Then McCall knew why Kettle wore that suit with the droopy coat sleeves: the man suddenly snapped his right arm down and forward and a twin-barrelled der- ringer shot out of the sleeve on a spring-loaded harness into his waiting hand.

McCall dived for the floor, as the derringer boomed. *Big calibre*, he thought, and a ball burned his left side, high up, spinning him. His Colt roared twice and Kettle was flung violently across the table.

He rolled off and flopped to the floor, not three feet from where McCall lay, hand pressing into his wound. Kettle stared into McCall's face with wide, pain-filled eyes. 'He – He never said you – was so damn – fast!'

McCall covered him but the Colt felt heavy, the barrel waving back and forth. 'Which one paid you to kill me?'

'Fr-Frenchy. He seems to have – lotsa cash. Thinks he's bought Kane. Oh, sure, Kane'll see nothin' happens to him. Leastways, not till there's a chance for him to – to – get his hands on the dinero.'

McCall grunted, surprised it wasn't Kane who had set up his murder. He struggled to a sitting position, leaning gratefully against the log wall for support. 'You're never gonna collect your share, Kettle.'

'I know, I shoulda finished you soon's you showed. . . . Figured I could bleed a mite more outta you Now you've . . . done for . . . me.'

'Be happy, you're gonna die rich. Come on, you know a lot more'n you've told me. What's their plan? I want it all, and in detail.'

Kettle remained silent. 'You're gonna . . . be . . . disappointed you . . . sonuver. . . .'

He stopped as McCall cocked the Colt.

'You're dying, Kettle – in a lot of pain – But you ain't dead yet. . . . Think about that.'

CHAPTER 8

DARK TRAIL

Sergeant Gavin Darnley swore as he rammed the field glasses back into their leather case on his saddle. Then he wheeled his panting, sweating mount and spurred back down the slope toward the waiting troop.

They had dismounted by a waterhole and Captain Greer was packing a pipe, standing in the meagre shade of one of the few trees. He puffed a cloud of aromatic smoke and glanced up as he heard the swift tattoo of Darnley's mount's hoofs. He frowned, seeing how the sergeant was lashing with his rein ends, the horse stretching out, showing a little stagger after the long patrol. He jumped as his match burned down to his finger, shook it out and dropped it as Darnley came skidding in. A tall man, he straightened to full height.

'Sergeant! That's no way to treat your mount after the crossing we've just made! What d'you think you're. . . ?'

Darnley swallowed and rose in the stirrups, pointing back up the rise. 'That smudge of smoke. Cap'n—' He had to fight for breath. 'It's the Mission! Los Pobre! She's burned to the ground, fire dyin' now, looks, looks to be a lot of bodies! At least twenty.'

Greer stared, holding his pipe a few inches from his mouth, not noticing that the tobacco hadn't caught properly.

'Right! Get the men mounted, unsheath rifles and sabres. We ride in battle formation!'

'Yessir!' the Sergeant snapped a salute, muttered to himself as he rode across to where the troopers were lounging around the waterhole. *Form up! Goddamn Officer School and their book learnin! We oughta go in like a buffalo stampede full tilt. But 'Form up', he says. Like we're in a goddamn inspection parade! – Greenhorn!*

'Mount up! Mount up!' he roared, the men stirring now when they saw the state he was in. 'Weapons unsheathed – ready to fight!'

'Fight who, Sarge?' someone called.

'*Fight*! That's all you need to know! Pronto!'

The troop rode up the slope in ragged form and Darnley could see by Greer's face that the man was going to tear a strip off him as soon as they reached the top of the slope. He headed it off, by, literally, heading off the Captain.

'Sir, you should prepare yourself, I used the glasses an' it ain't a pretty sight, sir.'

'Stand aside, Sergeant! I am prepared for any situation.' He took out his field glasses and lifted them to his eyes as they topped-out properly, adjusting focus.

Darnley smiled thinly when he saw the man's knuckles whiten as he suddenly gripped the glasses hard enough to crack the lenses. Then, a horrified whisper: 'Oh, my *God*! Those blasted red *devils*!'

Darnley could have said something a lot stronger but stayed silent. He thought – *hoped* – Greer was about to throw-up, but the captain gained control, face white now as he signalled the troop to close up on the crest.

'I-I will lead, Sergeant.'

Darnley felt a surge of unexpected approval at that, set his horse to one side and slightly behind Greer as the stiff-backed officer waved on the troop, riding at their head pistol in hand, towards the blackened, smoking smear that had once been the largest and most popular Mission in the Cherokee Strip. . . . It had been run by an Irish Catholic priest named O'Halloran, with two Irish nuns and people of any nationality who would volunteer for work.

There was always a group of ailing, poor people – some came all the way up from Mexico because of O'Halloran's well-known benevolence – and they tended vegetable gardens, repaired buildings and kept the church in splendid condition.

Now it was all gone.

Reduced to piles of charred, smoking timbers, collapsed adobe walls, slaughtered farm animals – and slaughtered people.

Mutilated bodies lay everywhere – the poor, the volunteers, the nuns and the monks. There were only three of these, plus O'Halloran himself. It took a little time to decide which corpse was his – normally he would be easily recognized by his thick thatch of silver hair – but he had been scalped. As had every other body, even the four children. Captain Greer was pale and his face was sweaty, but he did not shirk his duty. He examined every corpse with his sergeant, made notes. There was nothing to identify anyone, only the engraved silver crucifix still clutched in the big hand of Father O'Halloran.

'Wonder how the murderin' bastards missed that?' mused Darnley aloud.

Greer mopped his face yet again with his yellow neckerchief: it was already sodden with his perspiration. 'As you know, Sergeant, I'm a man not given to profanity, but I must concur with your description of the – whoever did this.'

'Indians, sir. Renegades and breakaways from the Reservations, I'd guess. Always a lot of discontent up there. . . . We found a couple of arrows, mangled some, a bloody tomahawk, and part of a vest with some heathen paintin'. Hard to say which tribe . . . likely drunken bucks from all over.'

He paused as Greer made some notes in his black, leather-covered book, hand shaking a little.

'I'd like to be in any punitive patrol you put together, Captain.'

Greer raised his eyes slowly. 'There will be no such patrol, Sergeant, until we are certain who perpetrated this.'

'Aw, Cap'n, you ain't never gonna pin it down *exactly*, sir! Ain't enough to go on. . . . A damn good purgin' through all them Injuns livin' off the Gov'mint handouts'll make 'em think twice about pullin' anythin' like this again.'

'Thank you, Sergeant. I'm sure Major Usher will be interested in your suggestion. For now, arrange a burial detail and. . . .'

Cap'n, sir!' The lookout posted on a rise, called down, waving his arms. 'Rider comin', sir, leadin' a hoss with what looks like a body draped over it. . . .'

Darnley didn't wait for orders, ran to where the lookout was and took the field glasses the man handed him. The sergeant focused quickly, adjusted again and the trooper noticed how Darnley tensed.

'By Godfrey. That looks like Josh McCall!'

It was. And McCall rode in twenty minutes later, covered by the guns of a couple of troopers, others crowding around to look at the man roped over the second horse.

'Who we got there, Josh?' Darnley asked after they had shaken hands.

'Vern Kettle. You know him?'

'That two-timin' son of a bitch! Hell, it's a wonder someone din' shoot him years ago. You kill him?'

'I shot him. Figured he was dying, but he's tougher than I reckoned and the bullet didn't do as much damage as I thought. I – er – got a little information out of him I needed, was gonna leave him, but figured I'd have to pass the Mission here on my way and reckoned if he lived that long, I'd leave him for the priests to take care of him.'

'Should've left him to die. He's gotten a lotta men

killed. Not all stand-up citizens, but he's a snake!'

'Well, he'll be a dead snake soon, I guess.' McCall gestured to the ruins and the troopers digging a mass grave. 'Injun raid, I suppose?'

'Yeah – well, that's what we were figurin' but – I just got a good look at the hoofmarks: they were ridin' shod horses . . . which ain't very damn likely as you know. They're allowed to trap mustangs an' break'em, but not to shoe 'em.'

McCall narrowed his eyes, looking around slowly.

' 'Nother thing,' Darnley added. 'Father O'Halloran had a lot of silver and gold stuff for the altar – brought it from Ireland. . . . Well, we found a couple half-melted brass crosses but no signs of the other stuff. . . .'

'If you're saying it was whites, and they took the valuables, there's only one bunch I know who'd do this.'

Darnley nodded slowly. 'Yeah! The Scattergun Gang! Josh, Kane'd be capable of doin' this. But why the hell would he? We heard he was runnin' scared well to the east of here. Major's orders were to check out the Mission and the Preacher's and the odd tradin' post set-up in here, then swing into the search for Kane. General feelin' is, he's already made it across or is hidin' deep in the Territory. We brought enough supplies to spend a few weeks flushin' him out.'

'Kettle said Kane's running for Mexico.'

Darnley swore. 'He sure has a hot potato up his ass, all right! But we'll catch up with the sonuver before he gets that far!'

'Aims to use the riverboats, according to Kettle. You know he's got some Frenchman with him who's suspected of being the one tried to kill the President, don't you?'

'Yeah, that's why the Major sent us on this patrol but I guess he figured Kane'd hole-up *in* the Territory.' He jumped as Kettle gave a grunt and one leg kicked slightly. 'Jesus! I was thinkin' he was dead by now!'

'You got a doctor with you?'

'Sure, but I was gonna say he'll be mighty busy here, but these folk only need a preacher – and a grave.'

They both turned as there was some obvious excitement near the bullet-chipped stone steps of the Mission building, which led to the crumbling entrance. Two troopers were carrying out a body, horribly burned, the raw, scalpless head glistening in the sunlight after the gorging flies erupted in a dark cloud. One trooper coughed and yelled and dropped his end of the burden.

'Careful!' snapped Captain Greer.

'Sounds like they've found someone still alive!' Darnley wheeled and started across, McCall following.

It was one of Father O'Halloran's monks. The men made him as comfortable as they could and the army doctor hurried up with his valise, knelt, and began to work over the dying man. He turned and looked up at Captain Greer.

'You won't get anything out of him, Captain. He's close to death and, besides, the monks here all take a vow of silence. They never even pray aloud.'

The doctor paused as charred, raw and peeling fingers tugged weakly at his jacket sleeve. He gulped and placed a hand on the man's badly burned forehead.

'Rest now, friend. I'll do what I can to make your passing a little easier but, well, you know you'll soon meet your Maker, don't you?'

The man stared with eyes McCall was sure couldn't see anything, not with those terrible burns. Then, along with the others who had gathered round, he stiffened as guttural, unintelligible sounds came from the monk's throat.

'My God! He, he's trying to *speak*!' exclaimed the doctor. 'Captain, this has to be almighty important, for him to break his vow of silence – even though he's dying.'

Greer knelt, taking that awful charred hand between his own, patting gently. The soldiers exchanged glances at their Captain's display of compassion. He spoke quietly.

'Brother, we are listening. . . . You have great courage and I'm sure the Good Lord would want you to help us see your tormentors get their just desserts. . . .'

He signed irritably for everyone to be quiet, to stop moving, almost to stop *breathing*, as he leaned forward and placed his ear against the lipless mouth.

His face changed expression many times and when the burned man finally gave the death rattle, Greer straightened, very pale, but obviously making an effort to stay in control.

'Pardon me,' he said politely, lurched away and vomited behind a boulder. He came back, obviously shaken, and Darnley proffered a canteen of water.

The Captain rinsed his mouth, nodded to Darnley as he handed the canteen back, then looked at the expectant faces.

'I couldn't make out hardly anything he said. Mostly it seemed to be about "habits" – his vows no doubt preying on his mind – and he mentioned "Father" twice. He could've been talking about God or just O'Halloran: in fact I think he said "cassock" once. I'm afraid his mind was gone. He must've been terribly worried about breaking his vows.' He looked at the corpse, now covered with a saddle blanket. 'Rest in peace, my friend. You did exceptionally well.'

'Nuns' robes're called habits.'

All eyes turned to McCall as he made the comment.

'What the devil has that to do with anything?' snapped Greer.

'He might not've been thinking so much about himself and breaking his vows. He might've been talking about the others who'd lived at the Mission. You said he mentioned cassock: that must've been referring to O'Halloran. . . .'

'Ye-es, possibly. But it makes no nevermind now, does it? There was nothing to help us.'

'He must've been trying to tell us something.' Greer frowned at McCall's insistence. 'Well, think about it – a man in that condition, burned to a crisp – breaking a solemn vow which meant more than life itself to him – he must've been trying to tell us something, Cap'n.'

The Captain's mouth tightened. 'Are you saying I didn't pay enough attention to that, that ghastly garble?'

'No, sir – I'm just saying he made that huge effort – so, must've been some reason driving him. . . .'

The Captain's face straightened and he nodded slowly. 'You may be right. But I can't see past the few words I was able to pick out – habits, cassock – what *could* he have been trying to make me understand. . . ?'

No one had any idea. Then—

Greer's voice suddenly strengthened and his mouth hardened. 'But I swear before every one of you, I will run down the people who did this – atrocity! I will see to it that they are punished to the full extent of the law.'

'Not if I get within gunshot!'

The anonymous voice spoke from the middle of the crowd of troopers and there were murmurs of approval, although Greer roared, 'who said that!' He waited, but, of course, there was no reponse. 'Now, I want it understood that there will be no summary justice here! We are representatives of our government and *we will uphold the letter of the law*!' Narrowed, cold eyes raked the uncomfortable ranks of dusty soldiers. 'We have a book of rules to work by – *and we will follow them! To – the – letter*! Do I make myself clear?'

There were a few murmurings but it was obvious Captain Greer would have to be mighty slick to stop a rifle firing 'accidentally' or a guard having to shoot a prisoner 'while trying to escape'.

McCall turned away to the horse where Kettle was draped. He was examining the man when Sergeant Darnley came up.

'He still breathin'?'

'Hard to tell, but I think he's still got a little life left in him. I'll leave him here, Gavin. Can you get me some grub – coffee, mostly, and some hardtack, mebbe a hand of sowbelly.'

Darnley nodded. 'You'll have to slip away quietly:

99

Cap'n knows you want Kane bad and after that leetle oath he took about doin' things by the goddamn book! Well, he'll want to make sure *no one* jumps the gun, civilian or soldier.'

'Can you keep him busy, after you get me some grub? Lug Kettle across and give him the man's history or something, divert his attention.'

'Yeah. Can do. But, Josh – I don't have to tell you, you're goin' up agin the worst bunch of killers ever to hit Texas – you take damn good care.'

'Rosa's still with 'em, Gavin.'

'Yeah – well, I hope so. . . .' He looked suddenly embarrassed. 'Hell, I din' mean that to slip out. . . .'

McCall's face was grim. 'I'm way ahead of you. But while Rosa's my main objective, I still want Kane no matter what . . . more so, if anything's already happened to Rosa.'

'Wish you luck.'

McCall started to turn away but swung back, looking puzzled.

'One thing before you go, Gav. No one's ever said who that other woman is with Kane.'

Darnley shook his head. 'Dunno, pard. Just some whore, I guess.'

McCall nodded almost absently: but it seemed to him that maybe it was a question that should have been asked long before this.

At least he had a fresh trail to follow: the raiders hadn't bothered to cover their tracks. Which likely meant they were in a hurry, were working to a timetable, maybe.

But, if so, why did they stop off here for this mas-sacre. . . ? Were they after something besides a little gratuitous blood-letting? he wondered, as he walked his horse behind some boulders, out of Greer's sight.

Once clear of the activities still going on at the Los Pobre site, with the bulk of the rise to shield him, McCall scouted around and found the mess of tracks that had to be those left by the raiders when they quit.

They were headed in the general direction that would take them to the Brazos – and the tracks were the same as those he had been following for days . . . no doubt.

The Scattergun Gang.

CHAPTER 9

NOW AND THEN

It wasn't long before McCall knew he had been had.

Moving away from Los Pobre, the gang had ridden in a tight formation, heading for the Brazos. But they scattered when they reached country that was largely broken, rearing slanting walls, angled slopes that ended abruptly, then dropped away sheer, nowhere to go. Aeons ago, there had been violent volcanic disturbances here, shifting tectonic plates, throwing up or shattering others, spewing lava in rivers and cooling mushroom-shaped mounds, changing the plains into a madman's maze of almost impassable country. Many of the hills and buttes were now covered in grass or brush or timber, deceptive, dangerous for the unwary.

It was a dizzying cluster of snake-like passes and arroyos – and when he found himself back in a big, half-circle draw he had crossed hours earlier, he knew they had tricked him.

Not him specially, perhaps, but anyone who followed – and they must know there would be someone: army, a posse under Sheriff Tim Blood, or even one led by a US Marshal, but there would definitely be pursuit.

So, they had naturally taken precautions – and he had been so eager to make up for lost time, he hadn't given enough thought to how Kane would be thinking.

The outlaw had out-distanced and outsmarted every posse that had pursued him. Some he and his killers had shot to ribbons, others he had steered into inhospitable country and abandoned them, after taking all their food and guns.

But he was always in control, even when it seemed just the opposite, that he had finally been run to ground. . . . It hadn't happened so far – and there were few still alive who could tell about the bloody ambushes the Scattergun Gang had set up.

Josh McCall didn't aim to ride into one if he could help it.

He figured the gang had split-up but would rendezvous at some pre-arranged place. Meantime, he was really lost, angry at himself for allowing his present predicament to happen. Normally he was good at trailing, was alert to all kinds of dangers and sudden changes of direction. He rode without having to consciously think about it: someone once told him he had an innate sense of direction and, without any ego involved, he believed it was true. Now, perhaps he had been too cocksure and had blundered.

Not that this was the first time he had been truly lost, though there hadn't been many such occasions. But he had learned a long time ago, that if a man was completely disoriented, then primeval fears stirred within, causing panic if not controlled quickly enough.

So he hunted up a good slab of dark, cool shade, sat back against a rock and built a cigarette, at the same time noting that his tobacco supply was dwindling; something else he had overlooked! It was time to take stock: he recognized the gnawing feeling inside himself, the sudden wrench of belly, a brief instant of blurred vision, or accelerated heartbeat.

Not panic, but on the same road that could lead there: nor was it hunger. It was *anxiety* rather than worry, the curse of anyone with a halfway active imagination.

Rosa was his life, had been ever since she had dragged him out of the depths of alcoholism he had been floundering in: fighting, brawling, making a nuisance of himself, stealing small change just to buy a drink, once, even taking a half-gnawed bone from a dog when he had nothing else to eat. He had seen the inside of many local jails, worked a chaingang or two, been beaten-up and once, sinking to the lowest level in order to get a quick stake, *doing* the beating-up. . . .

Nothing to be proud of in those years. Nothing. . . .

Rosa hadn't bullied him, made him feel ashamed or done any of those things distraught relatives of drunks tried in desperate efforts to bring them back to their senses.

She hadn't even had experience with booze-artists: she just had an in-built empathy that seemed to guide her and it made him *want* to please her – eventually realising the only way to do that was to get off the whiskey.

It was only at that point, when he had made his decision, that she had asked him *why*. . . .

At first, he felt that clenching in his belly, the shutter coming down like a blind in his brain, hiding the memories. Then, to his surprise, for the first time, he felt like telling someone *why* he was making such a fool of himself.

He started but checked after a few words, *it didn't sound like a good enough reason, not to him!* But she had nodded encouragement for him to continue.

'It's time for you to put it all behind you, Josh. You've punished yourself for long enough.'

That was the difference with Rosa: when he had occasionally stumbled out a few halting explanations in the past – and given up quickly – the listeners had, without exception, tried to make him feel ashamed, endlessly pointing out the unhappiness he had brought to others by his drunken behaviour. It was true, of course: he had lost many friends, estranged his only sister and her family, couldn't keep a job much longer than it took him to earn enough for a bottle. . . .

Rosa had changed it all.

He found himself sitting down in her small kitchen, more sober than he had been for months, and taking a damned good look at himself.

She made him see early-on that he was not the first man to lose his young bride, certainly not the first, at the tender age of twenty-two, to have been forced into marriage because of an unwanted pregnancy.

105

At first he had refused Linda, saying, truthfully, that there was no way she could say with certainty that *he* was the father of the child she claimed to be carrying. . . . She was a popular topic of conversation in the bunkhouse and most other places where cowhands gathered.

But she was adamant and her two brothers, Seth and Rob, had tried to convince him in the alley behind Casey's saloon.

'Sis wants *you*!' Seth, the biggest, had told him. 'You're a top hand, got good prospects, and me and Rob aim to see our sister makes a good life for herself.'

'Not with me.' McCall had been adamant and the fists flew. He was a good brawler but Rob had brought a sock full of pebbles and he had come off second best.

Instead of making him agree to the marriage, it got McCall mad and when he recovered from the beating – and found himself without a job, the rancher's wife being narrow-minded when she heard the reason for his injuries – he went after the brothers. This time it was settled with guns.

McCall hadn't thought much about fast draws but discovered he had a natural talent for it, his first shot killed Rob where he stood and Seth panicked and ran, shooting wild, bullets flying all over Main. McCall chased him and cornered him behind the livery where Seth pretended to surrender but produced a pocket pistol and shot McCall in the side. McCall triggered instinctively and Seth died where he fell.

Businessmen were irate because some of the wild shots had smashed storefront windows or otherwise damaged their premises, endangered people. He had to clear town and was told never to return. So he hit the trails to the wild towns and Linda followed him. Her tears wore him down: she was alone in the world now that he had killed her only kin; the baby would grow up without a father: she knew she wouldn't be able to cope, trying to care for the baby, support them both. . . .

Feeling sorry for her, McCall married her and claimed a quarter-section under the New-Settlement Programme. He built a cabin, completed it well within prove-up time and he started to feel some pride in what he had accomplished. Then Linda told him one day the doctor said there were complications: her pelvis was small and it would be a difficult birth, may well be necessary for her to go into a hospital in one of the big cities. . . .

They had never been *happy* in the true sense of the word but it had been a reasonable arrangement after McCall had learned to ignore Linda's unreasonable demands.

But this had him really worried: he had convinced himself by then that the child was probably his and he was looking forward to the birth: *his own son or daughter!* But – a *hospital!* How could he possibly afford that?

Then on a night of wild storms Linda had woken in the lightning-streaked darkness, screaming she was dying, '*The pain! Oh, Lord – the terrible pain!* Do something, get a doctor – get out and saddle a horse. No, don't leave me alone. *Oh, oh* Help meeeee!'

Her pleas and cries of genuine agony set him saddling the fastest mount he had in the small corrals – a half-broke buckskin with a wild, rolling eye. He dosed Linda with hot coffee liberally laced with whiskey and she was quieter, sleepy, when he quit the cabin and raced through the lashing rain and winds powerful enough to hurl full-grown trees around like a handful of flung matchsticks.

The horse fought and tried to bite his leg. He fought back with clenched fists, raking spurs and, finally, within sight of the hazy lights of town, the buckskin veered sharply for no apparent reason, and plunged into some trees.

A low branch swept him from the saddle, smashing him almost unconscious. The horse crashed away, whinnying wildly, into the fury of the night. . . . McCall eventually staggered into town, blood from a gash across his forehead almost blinding him. He literally pulled the sawbones out of his bed, harnessed a team to a flatbed wagon, then, with the furious medico, started back towards his land – and Linda.

They were too late – found her on the floor, some of the bedclothes, now sodden with her blood, tangled around her legs, the mattress sagging over the bed frame.

No amount of reassurance could convince McCall that it had not been his fault: *if only he had gone to town earlier when Linda first started complaining, if he hadn't chosen the half-wild buckskin, if he hadn't lost time trying to cross the swollen creek instead of taking the longer trail to the regular ford. . . . If.* The list tore on through his tortured mind: he had wiped out a whole family, Linda, Seth and Rob – and the baby, possibly *his* child – killed them all!

For a man with McCall's strong sense of responsibility it was too much blame to carry around – but he found it a mite – just a mite – easier after a few drinks.

Then the few became many and finally reached the stage where one drink was too many, but a hundred not enough. . . .

How he survived those next six years was a mystery. Booze had him in its grip and he sank to the lowest levels. But he knew he had to have money to buy booze – so he drove himself to work on days when he only felt like crawling into a grave – *any* work: menial tasks – saloon swamper, livery stable cleaner, trash pit digger – not realizing, nor caring. he was unconsciously keeping himself at such a low level of existence – he figured it was all he *deserved*, anyway.

And then he met Rosa, when he had reached an all-time low, having broken into her cabin behind her dressmaking shop, looking for liquor or money or items he could sell. . . .

She caught him, a gun in her hand, held in such a manner that it convinced him she knew how to use it and had the will to do so if he was stupid enough to give her trouble. . . .

But, weak from hunger, debilitated by alcohol and lack of even basic health care, he collapsed at her feet. . . .

Next he knew he was in a bed with clean sheets and he was clean, too. That startled him but Rosa soon put him at his ease, fed him, cared for his wants – and *saved his life*. That was the only way he saw it and would have it no other way: without her, he would have died and a

109

long-buried pride re-asserted itself so that he swore a silent oath that he would really make the effort, sober-up, take care of himself and find steady work.

Make her proud of him so all the efforts she was expending on his behalf would not be wasted. . . .

Six months later, still sober, with added pounds on his tall frame, and a poker win that allowed him to buy a small section of land, he had gone back to that town and married Rosa. . . .

They had had two happy years together: he was struggling to build-up the ranch now, but he could do it and would. He had found happiness he never knew existed. . . .

Then Kane and his killers had come along, robbed the Jacksboro Bank – burned his spread and taken Rosa. . . .

There wasn't anything in this life that would prevent him from finding her again – and squaring things with Kane – *nothing could stop him.*

As if to prove it, as he mashed out the cigarette against the rock, he looked up, glimpsed the sun between the high walls that seemed to want to topple in on him, and, when he saw the rim's shadow, suddenly, he knew which way to go.

In just under two hours, he had cleared the mad maze and was skirting the broken area, looking for tracks. He found them just before sundown at a pair of twin boulders.

Kane was playing it smart again: earlier, McCall had isolated a set of tracks from the others, ones he figured were made by Rosa's mount – they could have been made by the other woman, but he was a man who followed strong hunches. The rider was lighter than the roughnecks who followed Kane and it showed in the hoofprints, not so deep as the men's: thinking positively he decided they were made by Rosa.

But now there were no lighter tracks – they were *all about the same depth.* It took him only a short time to realise there was a set of hoofprints that were bigger than the others, indicating a large horse. So he figured Kane had made Rosa change mounts. A careful search and he found the sign he had seen earlier and called 'Rosa's', but although the shoes had the same marks – a bent nailhead, a chip out of a leading edge – they were now made by a heavier rider.

If Kane reckoned this would throw McCall into worry and indecision – he was right. But McCall pushed on, following the trail left by the bunch who had separated back at those twin rocks and who were now heading due east. The other bunch were moving almost south east, but he decided they were both probably aiming to end up at the Red River, just taking different trails.

Earlier, he had decided that the talk and sign Kane had planted, involving the Brazos, were deliberately misleading – it simply didn't make sense to add all that distance if, as he believed, they were eventually making for Baton Rouge or New Orleans. If he was wrong—

Well, he didn't want to think about that. . . .

He ate hardtack washed down with creek water for supper and turned-in early.

He was on the trail again in the half-light of pre-dawn, all guns oiled and fully loaded, headed for the many rivers he had to cross in this section of the Badman's Territory.

Moving steadily, relentlessly, towards Kane and his Scattergun Gang!

If they lost him or out-distanced him, he would find their trail again, follow them all the way down into Mexico if he had to.

They didn't know it, but there was no escape as long as he lived.

CHAPTER 10

RED RIVER RIM

He chose the wrong bunch to follow.

It didn't become obvious to him until he crossed a river he took to be the Red – it was, but it was the *North Fork* of the Red River – too far north of where he figured they would cross before turning south.

Even so, it wasn't the trail that gave them away, it was the gunfire.

He didn't know that when Kane had split the gang, he had paid-off the bunch that chose to ride south east.

Kane, looking more dangerous and blood-thirsty than ever after all this time living rough, faced the six men and chose to speak to Reed Hallam. Reed was a square man – in shape only: not in his dealings with others – and he liked killing, almost as much as he liked saloon gals. Make that 'gals in general' – with plenty of emphasis on the plural.

'Reed – You boys are eligible to share in that bank

money. Sure, we've lost a couple of the fellers who helped pull it off, but you've had to dodge lead, too, since you joined us, so seems only fair you should take their share.'

Hallam had no argument with that: nor did the others in his group, though they were more than a little suspicious at Kane's apparent generosity.

Straight to the point, Reed asked, 'How much?'

'I figure it at twenty-four thousand – give you four thousand apiece – Sound OK?'

Five men were eager, but became slowly solemn when Hallam pursed his lips doubtfully.'If you're givin' us that much, how much've you got comin'?'

Kane grinned tightly.'That's strictly between the Frenchman an' me – oh, and the other boys in my group.'

'How much?' Hallam insisted, and they all saw the friendliness fade swiftly from Kane's rugged features.

He shifted his feet slightly, seemed to loosen his shoulders, but made no move towards his gun – yet. 'Told you. Now, you happy with it, or not?'

'Not!' Reed Hallam snapped and reached for his gun.

Kane's Colt bucked in his hand, twice, three times. Hallam was blown back awkwardly over the uneven ground, collapsed on his belly. He tried to lift his head, but couldn't, and his last gasp was just strong enough to puff some dust from the ground under his face as he died.

Kane, still holding his smoking Colt, gave the staring men a tight, humourless grin.'Gives you fellers another

– what? – eight-hundred bucks apiece? I was you, I wouldn't have any argument with that.'

They didn't. He handed over the money, in a battered saddlebag, returned to where his own group waited.

'All settled, no real problems,' Kane told them. 'Let's go, it's a long way and that riverboat won't wait.'

The men were already mounted, crowding around the two women who still wore ponchos over their clothes despite the heat: on the Frenchman's orders.

No one spoke as they moved out, swinging due south now. . . .

McCall knew nothing about that, but he was struggling to make out some trail sign in the fast-fading light of late afternoon in this high-walled country when he heard a sound like someone hammering nails in the distance.

It was ragged, with short bursts of 'rapping', a pause, a single 'tap', then several more in an uneven pattern. He recognized the sounds for what they really were: there was a gunfight not too far away. Just as if to confirm it, he heard the double roar of a sawn-off shotgun – then silence. *Trademark of the Scattergun Gang!*

He stood quickly, climbed awkwardly to the top of an egg-shaped boulder, rifle in one hand. The echoes had died away by now, so he wasn't expecting a bullet that laid a streak of silver across the boulder not six inches from the hand he was resting on it.

As the lead screamed away, he dropped off the boulder, landing in a crouch, heard two more shots whine off the rock. Thumb on the rifle's hammer, he eased around the rock. The shots had come from up on the rim above his position. Rifle ready, he scanned the rim, slightly to his right. He saw movement, crouched lower, then half rose and levered and fired twice. He saw one bullet puff dust from the rock edge, then a man yelled, lurched half upright, scrabbled wildly, and slid, flailing, over the edge: he was either hit or had just lost his grip. He came rolling and bouncing down, scattering gravel, his rifle jarring from his hand.

He landed not six feet from McCall who waited, glancing up at the rim again. But there didn't seem to be any more danger from up there: but he saw what looked like an unmoving arm dangling over the edge several feet along.

The man who had fallen was hurt, winded, but still very much alive and trying to get his sixgun out. But he was half-lying on the holster, the weapon jammed in tightly.

'Leave the gun and crawl over here.'

'Wh-what? My leg's busted!'

'Hogwash. You're moving it while you're trying to get the Colt out. Now crawl over here, or die where you are.'

The man crawled over, gasping painfully and swearing, dragging an injured but unbroken leg behind. 'Judas! You – you're McCall, ain't you. . . ? We thought we'd lost you.'

'You're not that lucky. Who are you and what were shooting at?'

'Name's Wiley – Kane split us again – Tried to buy us

116

off with some of that bank money, but only the top couple layers were the real stuff, the rest crumpled paper.' He swore, rubbed his leg. His jaw was bleeding where he had banged it on the rock, and one hand was badly scraped.'Gimme some water, huh?'

'Finish what you were saying—' As the man's lips clamped, McCall prodded him with the rifle muzzle. 'Finish it, Wiley! Or I'll finish you.'

The outlaw gulped. 'There was an argument. Couple boys couldn't agree on how to split it. Others wanted to go after Kane – which was plumb loco – I run when they started shootin'—'

'Sure! And grabbed the money while they were busy.'

'No, no! Hell, you got it wrong—'

'Where is it? On the rim where you fell from?'

'I just told you I never—'

'You want that water, don't you? Well, it's gonna cost you – however much *dinero* is up there.'

'You sonuver! There's only a thousand, mebbe.'

The rifle barrel tapped him – not lightly – across the bridge of the nose and the man howled as blood flowed. 'How many left alive? Or didn't you wait to see?'

The now scared eyes lowered. 'I – din – wait. Mebbe two. They'd've killed me, I had to shoot first, and fast.'

'You'd've had lots of practice, riding with Kane. My wife still with him?'

McCall saw the cunning cross the man's beard-shagged face, then lifted the rifle slowly, placed the muzzle against his shoulder and cocked the hammer.

Suddenly the man was all nods and words. 'Yeah! Yeah! She's still there! With that other weird bitch.'

'And the Frenchman, you mentioned. He seems to be in charge. Were you at Los Pobre?'

The eyes avoided McCall. 'Er – no, I joined later.' He yelped and half lifted as the rifle pressed up under his jaw, foresight tearing into the graze already there. 'Don't! OK! I was there! We had to be. Frenchman's in charge – promised Kane a whole slew of money when they get to Baton Rouge. . . .'

He clamped his mouth suddenly, realizing he was giving away too much.

'That's a long ways from here, feller. You might as well tell me the rest. I'm real interested now and if you clam-up on me. How you spell your name, by the way?'

'Why. . . ?'

'Might take time to put a marker on your grave. . . .'

The man seemed to collapse in on himself. 'Look, you gotta b'lieve me. I dunno nothin' really – I'm in it for the money – nothin' more – I don't care who shot at the President – nothin' like that. All I know is Kane's bein' paid a small fortune to get the Frenchman down to Mexico. We all figure he's the one tried to kill the President.'

'What about the women? And you know which one I'm most interested in.'

Wiley looked really scared now, was almost cringing. McCall frowned briefly, then said in a hard voice, 'What's Kane got planned for the women, damn you?'

'I-I reckon you know. . . .'

'See how good a guess you can make.'

'Aw – Look, I-I ain't in that part! I been paid off – I – OK! Jesus, man, don't shoot me! All I know is the talk is

118

they're takin' a schooner across the Gulf, an' Kane's sellin' your wife to the White Slave market, figures he'll make a fortune, with that hair of hers. On top of what Frenchy's payin' him, he'll be able to live a real easy life.'

'That won't happen. But go on . . . why did you say he's turning Rosa over to the White Slavers? What about the other woman? And who is she, anyway?'

'Dunno. They call her Carmella, but I don't think it's her real name. She don't say much. Don't think she speaks much American. Talks like a Gatlin' gun to the Frenchy, though, in that frog lingo.'

'She's with him, then? Not just some whore Kane picked up. . . ?'

McCall said it thoughtfully, his puzzlement clear.

'Not sure. They kept us right away from her. An' your wife,' he added quickly.

McCall had other questions but he sensed this sorry son of a bitch wouldn't know the answers. 'Just one more thing, Wiley. If they're going down-river, it has to be by riverboat. Where're they boarding?'

'Not sure but – it has to be Shreveport, don't it?'

McCall nodded slowly. *Yeah – had to be. They've avoided the so-called 'Cowboy Crossings' that the trail herds use: Ringgold, Red River Station, Doane's Crossing, Denison's Ford.* Then he thought of something else.

'Why did the Frenchman want to wipe out Los Pobre?'

'Hell, don't ask me. Somethin' they did to him years ago, I think. We had to make it look like an Injun attack. We was only s'posed to take what was on the list he gave Kane, nothin' that could be traced back to the place.'

McCall frowned. 'You know what was on it? And you say "dunno" one more time, I'll loosen your teeth.'

'Well, I dun— I – wasn't told! But they said we could take the altar silver an' stuff unless it had Los Pobre stamped on it . . . only other thing seemed to be a bag of clothes.'

It sounded to McCall as if this Frenchman wanted to destroy the mission, but was taking measures to make sure he couldn't be connected with the massacre – or was it something else he didn't want his name to be connected with. . . ?

The answer had to lie in that list, and there was only one way McCall could get a look at that.

'Wh-what're you gonna do with me?' Wiley asked.

'You? First I'm gonna take your gun, tie you up, then climb up to the rim and see who's alive and who isn't. . . .'

'I lied. Ain't anyone up there now still livin' – but what about the money?'

'It might buy me some information I need.'

'Hey, listen! That's my money now! I—'

'Yeah, I know – you killed your so-called friends for it. I figure it's up for grabs, and I'm grabbing. You want to give me an argument?'

Wiley didn't.

'Your horses, where are they?' McCall asked suddenly, finishing off the knots on Wiley's wrists: the man would work free in time, but McCall aimed to be a long way from here when he did.

'Hosses? Back in a draw up there. Listen, you gotta leave me one if you're thinkin' of runnin' 'em off. This is God-awful country to cross.'

Scattering the horses wasn't what McCall had in mind. Maybe he'd turn a couple loose, but he needed at least three, with their saddles.

It was going to be a long, gruelling ride to Shreveport and it had to be fast – if he could transfer from one horse to the other on the run, he'd save a few minutes.

And from what he had buzzing around in his head right now, he knew every minute would count if he was going to save Rosa from the hell Kane had planned for her.

Then—

'Wiley, if Kane's running for Shreveport, to pick up a riverboat – how's he getting there?' The man looked blank and McCall snapped irritably. 'Is he riding all the way? Gonna try and grab a keelboat? What?'

Wiley frowned, held up his bound hands. 'Untie me – I – might be able to recall while you do it . . . OK?'

'Get your memory working now – I'll think about untying you when you remember.'

Wiley started to argue but the nudge of a none-too-tender boot toe in the ribs had him grimacing. Then he blurted:

'They met some feller told 'em the river's down. Not *flood* down, but dried up . . . shallow. So they ain't riskin' gettin' stuck on a sand bar in a keelboat.'

'Gonna ride overland all the way,' mused McCall half aloud and he almost smiled. 'Seems Kane don't know much about keelboats.'

He started for the slope up to the rim and Wiley yelled, 'Hey! Untie me!'

'You're soft, Wiley. You need the exercise. Won't take you more'n two or three hours to work loose. *Adios.*'

CHAPTER 11

THE RIVER

There hadn't been the usual Spring rains this season so far. Which meant the river, in places, was little more than a string of waterholes . . . news which had apparently scared-off Kane and his friends.

Normally, the smaller keelboats – not the large eighty-footers – still operated if the waterholes weren't too far apart. With a big enough crew *and* the passengers pitching-in, a fifty-footer could be dragged across the wet sand between waterholes – providing the cargo wasn't too large. Still, more than once twenty-five tons of bales and casks and other goods had been off-loaded while the boat was manouvered down-river, hole by hole. Killing work, but someone figured it had to be worth it. Competition was mighty stiff between the keelboat operators: some had connections with the bigger, cargo-carrying steamboats, stern-wheelers or side wheelers, that made it up-river as far as Shreveport.

And there were hazards, apart from the water itself: quicksand and snakes were often more of a danger than floods or strandings in the higher reaches.

McCall had no real idea what shape the river was in at this stage. Nor did he want to think about it. He had enough trouble negotiating the trails – or lack of them – that would take him down to one of the boat landings. He was making for Destiny which almost always had a deep-water anchorage – trouble was, waterholes above and below the landing weren't always co-operative: it had been known for a riverboat to be stranded for as long as three weeks before it could be re-floated.Which was one reason not many passenger-carrying boats operated at a profit north of Shreveport.

Kane must have heard about this and backed-off, choosing to make his run to Shreveport overland – longer, but more certain of getting there without too many delays.

Dragging the string of three horses behind the gallant old spotted grey, through twisting passes and climbing steep slopes he would never have considered attempting at another time, McCall had the recurring hope that the stern-or-sidewheeler Kane was making for would run aground or be delayed for some other reason.

But he was too practical to pin any high hopes on such a thing happening. If he didn't make Shreveport before sailing time, he would simply have to find fresh horses and race overland to the next port down-river, and make damn sure he was there waiting when the old steamboat came rumbling round the bend with its twin high smokestacks spewing a black fog across the Arkansas sky.

He had ridden a lot of bone-breaking trails in the past, but he knew these remaining forty miles to Destiny would take years off his life.

But it had to be done, if he wanted to get Rosa back.

And there was no question about that.

Nor the inevitable showdown with Scattergun Kane – and whoever else might try to stop him.

The captain of the sternwheeler, *Centurion*, was Lars Garrett, a big-bellied, bushy-bearded, ruddy-faced veteran of the river. He wore halfmoon glasses for reading, perched on the end of his veined, open-pored nose, and now set down the papers he was holding as Kane and *Monsieur* L'Vende awaited his answer to their offer. The Frenchman was dressed in a pale lavender split-tailed coat with darker silk edging, and striped trousers. His hair glistened with pomade and his thin moustache was perfectly trimmed. Kane was wearing his usual grimy trail clothes as well as a four-day stubble and his dust-red eyes were not friendly as he stared hard at the captain in the big cabin aboard the sternwheeler.

'Your offer is generous, gennlemen,' Garrett said, shaking his large head at the same time. Grey curls protruded from beneath the soft cap he wore, tarnished gold braid on the peak. 'But it is way below the value of this boat – and that's what I would have to replace if I sailed at the time you want.'

'It's only a day earlier than your schedule, for Chris'sakes,' Kane said in an unpleasant tone.

The captain's eyes were hard as he stared over his lowered spectacles. '*Only* a day! Spoken like a true land-lubber. A day can make one helluva difference, Mr Kane.'

'Yeah – it can. To us! An' we're willin' to pay for any inconvenience, so what's your problem?'

'Let me ask you this: can you arrange for the current to change a day early, Mr Kane? Can you get information about the condition of sandbars below Gresham Falls a day earlier? The silting rate of the approaches to Tricorne Bend – which takes twenty-four hours to monitor for results, by the way? No amount of money can hurry those things. And all are necessary for keeping this boat on schedule – and afloat! Dozens of people depend upon us being on time at certain places. You obviously haven't thought this thing through. If you had, you would see just how stupid your suggestion is.'

'Look, Cap'n,' Kane said in a forced, more reasonable tone. 'You've been workin' this river for – how long?'

'Since the late seventies, after they finally cleared the Great Raft.'

Kane blinked. 'What in hell is that?'

Garrett smiled indulgently. 'A massive natural log jam that took over ten years to clear and make the river navigible. It even backed-up thirty miles of Big Cypress Creek and formed Lake Caddo. It was cleared several times, every few years, but never permanently. That didn't happen until dynamite became freely available in the seventies.'

Kane broke in impatiently. 'Yeah, yeah, OK, I don't need no goddam lecture! Thing is, you've been on the river a long time. You got a good reputation, no major strandings or wreckings, So you're a man who knows this river back and forwards, right?' He gave Captain Garrett no chance to reply. 'So – just use your know-how to get over them little things you got buzzin' in your ear . . . and sail a day early!'

Garrett stood, his huge bulk seeming to cramp the office. 'Mr Kane, you're a paying passenger – You pay for my expertise and *my authority* . . . which, I might add, is on a par with God's once you step aboard my boat.' He paused to let that sink in, saw by Kane's bleak eyes his words had done nothing to appease the man. 'I must refuse all of your suggestions, but make one of my own.' He leaned towards the two men. 'You can take a refund of your fare – or wait for the sailing tide tomorrow forenoon as per schedule. . . . There are no other choices, gennlemen.'

Kane's mouth tightened and the Frenchman hurriedly stepped alongside and cramped Kane's gunarm as he started to reach for his gun. He shook his head briefly.

'*M'sieur L'capitaine.*' He added a slight bow. 'We, of course, accept your authority and knowledge – *Oui*, M'sieur Kane – *we* – accept!' He smiled at the big captain who stood there like a rock monument. 'We are impatient to see certain – friends in New Orleans, you understand – Ladies, of what I believe is called the *high-yaller* persuasion. . . ?'

Garrett gave a crooked smile. 'I understand. But

you'll just have to hold your impatience, *Mon-sewer.*'

'Of course! We also understand, but there is – still something you can do for us – *non, non!* Nothing that will affect your sailing schedule or the safety of your boat – just something for three of your passengers.'

Garrett was wary, but waited.

'We are offering—' L'Vende glanced at the surly Kane. 'Two – no, *three* hundred dollars . . . per'aps, five. . . ?'

'It comes outta your pocket,' growled Kane.

'Five hundred dollars, Captain, just to alter three names on your passenger list. . . ? It is worth your consideration, no?'

Captain Garrett was not fool enough to pass up a chance at lining his own pocket by agreeing to such a simple request. Of course, there had to be a catch but he also was in a bargaining position . . . as Kane had said, he knew this river, in more ways than one.

'Suppose I pour some brandy, gennlemen – and we discuss the details. . . ?'

'*Certainment!* Eh, M'sieur Kane?'

Kane grunted and waited for his drink, fingers tapping against his staghorn gun-butt while the Frenchman took out his wallet, smiling.

At least something seemed to be going right for them – it damn well better!

Josh McCall was also taking out his money pouch as he stood on the gangplank linking the battered old keel-boat to the bank of the Red River, far upstream from *Centurion.*

The man who accompanied him was one of the ugliest human beings McCall had ever seen, his face like a crumpled dishcloth – and about as clean – his lantern jaw jutting aggressively. But he had warm, almost friendly, eyes as he waited for McCall to hand him the money he had offered to pay for deckspace for himself and mounts on the fifty-footer.

The keelboatman's voice was raspy. 'You'll have to sleep with 'em, take care of 'em messin' on my deck – an' I mean clean it up right away, day or night.'

'I'll take care of it, Molina. Two horses, right? You supply a bale of hay.'

'Uh-huh – Deckspace and two hosses, plus feed – and I'll deduct a dollar for you doin' the cleanin'-up – say five bucks, plus your sleepin' space, that'll bring it to . . . lemme see. . . .'

'Too much, you damn chiseller!' But McCall smiled as he spoke and handed over the money, plus the extra five dollars for the piece of filthy, uneven deck he would be sleeping on – with luck. He had arranged for two mounts to come with him – in case there was a stranding and he could get ashore and ride the rest of the way to Shreveport – and hopefully be in time to catch the riverboat bound for Baton Rouge and New Orleans.

It wasn't the first time he had done such business with Molina. The ugly man was counting swiftly – having had lots of practice. 'If there's any shootin' or such—'

'There won't be,' McCall assured him. 'Not till I reach Shreveport.'

'If there's any on board you pay for the damages – if

you survive. If you don't, I'll take that poke off your corpse and dig you a grave on the nearest shore. . . . No mud. It'll be permanent an' won't wash away.'

'Oh, I'll appreciate that, Molina! When can we hope to get going?'

'If my last two oarsmen can be dragged outta that cat-house half-a-mile from the landin', we'll ride the current far as we can tonight. Enough moon for us to get a good ways downstream before mornin'. Mayhap without mishap!'

He laughed at his joke.

But the news was good for McCall. As long as Molina stayed sober enough not to run up on a sandbank or get stuck in quicksands.

He had to take a chance on that – even triple the money he had paid over couldn't guarantee it wouldn't happen.

Kane couldn't sleep. It wasn't that he was scared, though the strangeness of the riverboat and the endless thrashing of the huge sternwheel were alien sounds and he couldn't stay asleep, only cat-napped. The smell of hot oil and burning wood irritated him, gave him a headache which he tried to clear with a pint of whiskey, without much success.

Finally, he went up on deck and smoked a long cigar he had been given by Captain Garrett.

The brandy Garrett had served in his cabin this afternoon had been excellent: 'One of the, er, undisclosed benefits of the river trade,' he had confessed as the level in the bottle went down while the three of them made arrangements for slight alterations to the passenger list.

The Frenchman raised his glass, toasting the riverboat man. 'An excellent cognac for an excellent job, *L'Capitaine!*'

Garrett had had enough to enjoy the flattery, poured his own glass full again and tossed it down. 'You boys've got your own deal goin', I can see that, but—' He started to chuckle, shaking his head a little. 'But you see the joke in it, don't you? *Irony* I believe is the right word. . . . You told me you're chasin' a couple high-yaller asses in N'Orleans – well, you sure ain't the first to do that!' He emptied his glass and then, sniggering again, leaned across the table. 'But it's the first time I've heard of – *first* time I've heard of a priest footin' it after whores so, openly! Sure, sure, everyone knows what they say goes on in them con-vents an' missions with the Holy Fathers and the Nuns – *Un*-holy Fathers, I call 'em – but you two – you take the cake!'

He paused and jerked a thumb at the Frenchman. 'Well, *he* does.' He shook his head again in bewildered amusement. 'A priest an' two nuns goin' to a N'Orleans cat-house!' He clapped a big hand flatly on the table and the glasses jumped, Kane's spilling. 'If that don't beat all! Man, I'll never have to pay for a drink again, not for years, tellin' that yarn.'

He reared back as Kane lunged cross the table, the muzzle of his cocked Colt rammed up one huge nostril of Garrett's nose. The Frenchman grabbed Kane's arm but the wild-eyed killer threw him off effortlessly. He forced the big captain way back in his chair and was now almost kneeling on the man's barrel chest.

'Now that's just what you *ain't* gonna do, you fat bastard!' He screwed the gun into the nostril and blood oozed as the captain writhed and moaned. 'You savvy what I'm sayin'? You breathe one word of what's goin' on and you're dead, mister! *Dead!*'

'Keep your voice down!' hissed the Frenchman. 'Kane, we can attend to this later! It's all right now – eh, Capitaine? It is the cognac talking, eh? *Oui!* Of course – see, Kane, he understands.' The Frenchman's voice suddenly hardened. 'Don't you, Capitaine? You keep our private business very, very private. Or perhaps you have an accident, eh? A slippery deck near the sternwheel. Ah! I once saw a man who had fallen into such a wheel. It still makes me sick to recall.' He slapped the captain's fat, pale face, hard enough to sting. 'Thank you for your hospitality, Capitaine. We go to our cabins now and see you at breakfast – OK?'

Garrett said nothing, slumped in his chair, breathing hard and noisily, his eyes with a glazed look. Like a man in shock.

'Hell, I could've scared him so he wet his pants,' Kane said in a surly tone outside on the deck.

'I believe that embarrassing thing occurred, Kane. You are too unsubtle, *mon ami*. I had to be blunt with Garrett but I believe he will keep our little secret.'

'Yeah, He'll keep it all right. Permanently – after we get to Baton Rouge. . . . An' don't try to stop me this time, Frenchy, or you'll get a bullet before he does!'

Kane stalked away along the deck and the

Frenchman pursed his lips and rubbed his clean-shaven jaw gently.

A man to watch. No! A man who needed watching!

Kane had been drinking almost constantly since leaving the captain's cabin. He was harboring a growing hatred for Garrett.

The way the fat bastard had spoken to him! Giving him a *lecture*, for Chris'sakes! Treating him like a backward child. Well, only a very few men had ever done that to Kane and lived barely long enough to talk about it.

This one wouldn't.

Captain God Garrett! *We'll see, we'll see – You just get us down this lousy river and when we got no more use for you – you'll get your real payment!*

He drained the whiskey bottle and tossed it overside.

'Send you some company later,' he said and laughed to himself as he veered away to the ladder-steps leading to the cabins.

Lying on the hard, uneven planks of the keelboat's deck, head pillowed on his folded jacket, McCall slowly opened one eye. Greyness was all that he could see. No – he could make out some of the deck cargo, heard one of his mounts stomp and shuffle for balance as the boat rounded a bend.

Almost daylight, he thought and then realized he had been awakened by some other sound.

Not the monotonous squeak and *clack!* of the oars in their sockets as the crew of eight oarsmen hauled and pushed and pulled, some swearing as they sweated out a hangover.

None of those things. . . . He had *sensed* something rather than heard it: the old alert instinct for survival working in his favour. . . .

Hesitating no longer, he spun away to his left – again, by pure instinct: no time to reason it out – and his flailing arm hit something solid. Not a part of the boat, his brain registered instantly: *cloth, then hardness.*

A man's trouser-clad legs.

He bounded back the other way and there was a shadow suddenly blanketing him and something thudded into the deck inches from his head. Snapping his arched body like a bow, he bounced to his knees, palming up his Colt, and fired without hesitation at the shadow. A man spun away, yelling, and his companion started to turn to run but McCall shot him in the leg. He crashed, screaming, as the bullet shattered his shin bone.

Men were shouting as McCall straightened fully, smoking gun sweeping around as he saw the oarsmen shipping their long shafts, starting up out of their seats to see what was going on.

Only six at the oars. . . . Which probably meant the two he had gunned down were the missing oarsmen. He saw the empty seats with the shafts shipped, behind and one each side of the others. The six were menacing him now but the screams of the writhing, wounded man and McCall's gun held them back.

'You goin' over the side, mister.' growled a big, wide-shouldered man, stripped to the waist and with a faded

134

sailor's tattoo right across his chest: a large heart with the words *MOTHER* and *Billie-Jo* within its shape.

The men started forward and then the door of the only raised structure on the boat, at the stern – Molina's cabin – crashed open. Molina stumbled out wearing only a pair of loose trousers, hair awry, eyes reddened and mouth twisted with his huge hangover. He also had a shotgun and cocked both hammers as he swung it up, his friendly eyes decidedly unfriendly now.

The oarsmen stopped in their tracks, some looking mighty uneasy.

'Your own fault, McCall,' rasped Molina. 'Oughtn't've flashed that poke around. These men have sharp eyes.'

'You oughtn't've insisted I pay you out on deck,' countered McCall, still watching the others. He gestured to the man lying unmoving on the red-stained deck and the other groaning and thrashing about, splintered bone showing through his blood-soggy trouser leg. 'Guess you're short a couple of men now.'

'You can handle the steerin' oar, I'll take Morg's place.' He indicated the dead man, then glared at the bleeding one. 'Bandage that leg an' Connie can sit at his usual oar – ain't his arms that're hurt.'

'Jesus! I-I can't pull an oar! I'm *hurt*, dammit!'

Molina placed the shotgun muzzles against the back of the wounded man's head. 'Then I'll have to put you outta your misery, Con, just like I would a sick dog. What d'you say, eh?'

'*Wait!* – Oh, hell, Mol, I-I'm really *hurtin*'!'

'Yeah, time to put him down,' McCall said and

Molina pressed harder with the gun muzzles as Con spilled sideways in a dead faint.

'Ah, he'll pull his oar, all right,' Molina said. 'But we're gonna be slowed without two men who know what they're doin' – They're all part of a team, an' you've just busted it up.'

McCall cursed silently, almost ready to kick the unconscious man: *son of a bitch, just had to be greedy!*

Then he had a thought and looked hard at Molina: 'You figure you could keep to schedule – mebbe if you had a little more *dinero*, that it, Molina? That it. . . ?'

The ugly man tried to look innocent – an impossible feat. 'Ah, McCall! You know me! I wouldn't take advantage of you that way.'

'The first thing you said is right – I know you!'

Molina pursed his lips, the shotgun wandering about but pointing more in McCall's direction now. 'But since you put the thought in my head, mebbe another couple hundred'd help. Sling in an extra fifty for Con's leg. There're quicksands not far downstream, so we won't worry none about Morg. Save you some money.'

'You're a sly sonuver, Molina!'

'Well, you told me that was money you'd picked up from Tonto Wiley an' he never earned an honest dollar in his life. Don't hurt to share that kinda loot around – sure not when you're wantin' somethin' special yourself. . . .'

McCall almost shot him, but he had to have Molina to get the damn keelboat down-river in time to at least be within sight of Kane's riverboat at Shreveport – or however far down river it had already travelled.

He was closing the gap, but couldn't afford any more delays or Kane – and Rosa – would be on a schooner across the Gulf. . . . He gritted his teeth at the thought.

Then Molina spoke:

'We gotta deal?' The keelboatman didn't even sound impatient: he knew there was only one answer McCall could give.

CHAPTER 12

TAKE-OVER

There were about twenty passengers on the *Centurion* and every last one of them must have wondered about the sudden appearance of a tall padre accompanied by two petite nuns on the throbbing decks of the stern-wheeler as it thrashed its way down-river at a good rate.No one had seen them come on board. . . .

The whistle pierced the sunlit air with powerful jets of steam at every bend, as the big lumbering boat followed a serpentine path of channels deep enough to be navigible. The barren shore gradually gave way to clumps of trees: forests that one day would qualify as 'National Monuments'.

The only problem, if it could be called that, was that the Mate, and Garrett's only 'officer', had an accident in the engine room – one of the massive crankshafts had apparently struck him on the back of the head and he was knocked unconscious – hours ago, and was still out of it. Captain Garrett suspected a fractured skull – and that the 'accident' was no accident at all. The man was what was known as a 'Downeaster bastard', a brutal ex-whaler and sealer who, although an excellent seaman, used fists, feet and even illegal cudgels on the coloured engine room crew. Seemed to Garrett that someone saw a chance to pay-back – and though he had little sympathy for the mate, it meant the entire burden of navigation and general running of the *Centurion* had now fallen upon his shoulders. He would have to sketch charts ahead of time for the helmsmen – and some were unreliable, but finding a crew for the riverboats these days, with such low pay was difficult. A man had to take what he could get.

None of this did anything to sweeten his mood: he was red-eyed from lack of sleep, with more long hours on the bridge to come. . . .

The religious trio were not on deck for long at any time: and they looked genuine in the cassock and habits taken from the smoking ruins of Los Pobre. Kane, usually with another man named Yorke, trailed them, constantly watching for curious folk who might try to approach and start a conversation.

Kane himself, cleaned-up now and looking presentable in decent clothes, forced a smile and touched a hand to the brim of his hat as he stepped in front of a couple who were obviously ready to approach the padre and the nuns.

' 'Mornin', *amigos*. Sorry, but you can't talk with the Holy Father nor the nuns.'

The man, well dressed with a tall beaverskin hat drew

himself up. 'And, why, pray, shouldn't we. . . ?'

Kane wanted to say *Because I damn well said so!* but kept his smile in place with difficulty and explained: 'They've all taken a vow of silence.'

The woman, plump-faced and with high red spots on her cheeks, grabbed the arm of the man in the beaver-skin hat.

'Oh! Marvin! How exciting!' She flicked wide blue eyes toward Kane who tried not to show his impatience and dislike for these rich folk. 'What was the – situation, sir, that made them take such a – a burdensome vow?'

'I dunno, ma'am. All I know is I have to see no one disturbs their – er—' He groped for the word, but the woman was eager to help him out.

'*Communion* perhaps?'

His smile stiff, Kane nodded. 'You got it, ma'am. They're in *communion* with their God, I expect.'

'Surely you mean *everyone's God*, my man?' corrected the man haughtily.

It was too much for Kane and he dropped all pretense, even edged a hand towards his gun-butt. 'Whatever I mean, mister, it's best said like this: stay right away from 'em! Or I'll toss that silly damn hat over side – and you after it.'

'The captain will hear about this!' snorted the man and whirled the now tearful woman away.

Kane scowled, nodded to the silent Yorke and the big, hard-faced man stepped after the couple, walked close behind, forcing them, without laying a hand on them, to move off that part of the deck.

The Frenchman, sweating in his high collar and

black robe of the padre glowered at Kane. 'That was stupid, Kane!'

'Yeah? You wanna see stupid? Take a look in a mirror sometime.' He glanced at the two nuns, the square-faced one meeting and holding his gaze, face expressionless as usual – but a cold hatred showing in her slitted eyes. 'But youse ladies look real good.'

The other nun stood there, tightlipped, hands clasped in front of her, the cuffs of the robe covering her wrists so the silken cord binding them was not visible. Kane grinned, touched her white hood, laughed as she wrenched her head aside. 'Just makin' sure that valuable hair of yours aint showin', Cookie. . . . You look like you're prayin' with your hands in front like that. Good idea of mine, weren't it?'

'Just – leave me alone! I hate these clothes!'

'You look good in anythin', Cookie, you know that?' He winked at the Frenchman. 'Or in nothin', eh, Frenchy?'

The Frenchman hissed. 'You've been drinking!'

'And I'll be drinkin' heaps more before we get to Baton Rouge.' This time he winked at the nun he had called 'Cookie'. 'So I'll come see you later, Cookie – see if you can hang on to that "vow of silence" when I start on you.'

The Frenchman hurriedly stepped between Kane and the 'nuns', spreading his arms and ushering them away, throwing Kane a murderous look over one shoulder.

'Ah, go count your rosary beads, Frenchy.'

Then the square-faced nun said something short and

viciously in a language neither Kane nor Cookie understood. The Frenchman flushed deeply, and awkwardly bowed slightly to the nun. '*Pardon, ma'amselle!*'

Kane, lighting a cheroot frowned. *By hell, she sure bosses him around when she's riled – wonder what the deal is between them two. . . ?*

Miles upriver, the keelboat made a slow, weaving course through the string of waterholes. Once it seemed they would have to stop and maybe off-load some of the cargo, but Molina tongue-lashed the men, kicked one, and gave McCall a long pole which had obviously started out its days as a ten foot sapling. He picked up its twin and motioned McCall to stand a few feet from him on the port side.

'Push against the bank,' Molina grunted, demonstrating, the pole bending with his effort. 'Go on! Do the same – push *backwards*, damn you! *Forward's* the way we want to go, keep pushin' till I say stop!'

The keel scraped bottom and Molina got two more men to use their oars as thrusters, turning the bows slowly to starboard. Then McCall saw the sunken tree stumps just skimming by the hull, wondering how the ugly man had known they were there – they sure weren't visible until the boat was right on top of them.

He looked at Molina with more respect.

'We making – good – time?' he asked, still pushing with the long pole.

'Not bad – but we've got the Washboard to get over yet. If you're a prayin' man, say one that the water's high enough.'

'If it's not. . . ?'

Molina's face contorted and McCall realized the man was smiling – in his own way. 'You might be glad you brought them hosses.'

'I can get off and ride. . . ?'

'We-ell – was thinkin' more along the lines we might hitch 'em up to the bow an' let 'em haul us out. . . .' As McCall started to protest, he added quicky, 'Course, all depends on how bad you want to get to Shreveport. . . .'

'You sonuver!' growled McCall but he gave a crooked smile as he said it. 'And you charged me to bring those horses on your damn boat! Knowin' all along you'd likely use 'em!'

'What're friends for, eh . . . *amigo?*'

After supper, Kane was stretched out on his bunk, starting to doze, pleasantly warm and relaxed from all the whiskey he had been drinking.

The door opened and he suddenly snapped into action, rolling swiftly off the bunk, dropping to one knee, the cocked Colt in his right hand – covering the startled Captain Garrett who stood filling the doorway. The big man eased in far enough so he could push the door closed behind him.

'Easy now, Kane! Easy, man.'

'You'd do well to knock!'

'I can see that. You got time for a few words?'

'Fewer the better.'

'All right – straight to the point: there's been a – complaint, by several passengers. Important people from N'Orleans who you apparently insulted earlier.'

'That fat old bitch and the long streak of misery in

143

the beaverskin hat?' Garrett arched his eyebrows but nodded slowly. 'Forget 'em. They were tryin' to talk with the Frenchman and the nuns, was all.'

'I know – You'd've been wiser to explain in a less coarse and vulgar manner. Those people have breeding.'

'Look, Garrett – You don't scare me none, captain of this tub or not. You just get us to Baton Rouge, an' leave anythin' else to me.'

'That – sounds like a good idea, but, you see, I have to think beyond you disembarking at Baton Rouge – The *Centurion* is my livelihood. I have to ensure I keep the cabins full of satisfied customers, not ones who complain about being insulted and bullied.'

Garrett reared back as the Colt rammed into his big belly. Kane thrust his dark face close, reeking of booze. 'Go oil your engine – or chop some wood for the boiler, or somethin' – but *get the hell outta my cabin and leave me be!*'

'Damn you, Kane! You can't do what you like on board my boat. . . !'

'Betcha I can!'

The sound of the shot was muffled by the layers of Garrett's belly fat that bulged over the muzzle. The blast hurled the Captain back against the wall, his jaw dropping. Kane, unable to stop himself now his bloodlust was up, and too drunk to care anyway, screwed the gun in tightly against the bleeding belly and fired again, angling the barrel up this time. Captain Garrett made a choking, wet gargling sound and his legs began to fold under him. Kane stepped back to allow him to fall and stretch out on the floor.He leaned down over the dying man, pushed the pain-contorted face into the worn carpet and sneered, 'See. . . ?'

He reloaded the pistol, then went out, locking the door after him, going in search of Yorke. . . .

It would be full dark soon. They ought to be able to carry Garrett down to the stern and drop him over into the churning wheel. . . .

That way he'd be discovered, but the passage of the captain through the thrashing hardwood planks of the wheel would mangle his body and disguise the bullet wounds.

It would be recorded as *a tragic accident*. . . .

Kane felt mighty pleased with himself and decided to celebrate with a fresh bottle of whiskey after the job was done.

The only thing he hadn't thought of was who now would be able to navigate the *Centurion* through the maze of shallow channels and the stretches of quick-sand that lay ahead.

CHAPTER 13

BLACK WIDOW

It had to happen.

Captain Garrett had not yet been found, and the rough charts he had given the duty helmsman earlier took the boat only so far down-river. Garrett had probably intended to spend the hours after supper preparing more detailed directions as they dropped lower down the watercourse.

Instead, he spent the time in Eternity. . . .

There were plenty of hazards. Patches of quicksand clutched at the hull, only reluctantly releasing the slimy planks because of the greater power of the thudding engines. Shallows were a constant hazard – the silt was forever changing, filling up hollows here, scooping out holes there according to the vagary of the currents. Sometimes a small flood wave surged along the water course, ripping away the old banks, spilling mud and detritus into the right-of-way.

The discovery of Garrett's mangled body in the stern-wheel upset everyone. Now no one knew the best course.

No man could ever claim he 'knew' the river – there were too many potential dangers for that – but Captain Garrett had been as expert as anyone could get. Now he was nothing more than a heap of mangled meat wrapped in an old tarpaulin, deep in the hold of the *Centurion*. The stranding was more important right now than trying to find out how Garrett had fallen into the sternwheel: an investigation would be made later. The Mate was still unconscious and likely to die according to a doctor who was travelling as a passenger. The chief engineer, who spent more time in his cabin working over his beautifully detailed drawings of birdlife along the Red River, could offer little in the way of help for navigating the riverboat, or so he claimed. He could play his engines according to Garrett's orders in the difcult stretches of the river, but, deep in the thundering engine room, he could not say just where they were.

A small, rotund man named Cooney, who, from the rear, resembled an overweight child, was set in the bows, claiming he had rafted down this stretch of the river a few years ago, chased by rustlers. So far he had managed to signal in time when shallows appeared, but Cooney was not a tall man and his lack of height eventually let him down: he failed to see the swirl of currents that indicated shoal water as the *Centurion* lumbered around a tight bend. The bows crunched through rapidly shallowing water for several yards. Then the boat stopped as if it had hit a brick wall, splintering two small trees protruding from the muddy water, remnants of the Great Raft, in the process. The jolt threw Cooney overboard and as it was early in the day, spilled many passengers out of their bunks unceremoniously.

Kane and Yorke cuffed their way through the dazed crew, ignoring the floundering Cooney who eventually managed to stand up and wade towards ashore. Suddenly he screamed again, thrashing in panic, small, fat legs seemingly trapped in the sucking sand. He sank deeper with each wild struggle. Passengers and crew alike lined the rails. Two crewmen hastily threw out a line. But they were off target and by the time they were ready to throw again, Cooney had disappeared under the sludgy, semi-liquid sand, screaming mouth filling with oozing slush. . . .

Yorke, big and tough-looking as he was, paled at the sight. Women fainted, men gagged. Kane stared blankly, murmured, 'Looks like we ain't goin' ashore here.'

Several miles upstream, the keelboat was in similar trouble. But McCall's horses were already hitched to the bow and the cursing crew had unloaded much of the cargo, and were standing waist deep in the muddy water while McCall urged the horses to pull. Luckily there was no quicksand here.

Molina had his men use the long, hardwood oars as levers, rammed under the heavy hull in several places, timing their leverage with the forward-straining efforts of the horses, ropes and reins bowstring taut and thrumming as the men tried to break the suction.

It took more than an hour before they heard the sound they had been waiting for: the slurping, sliding release of the hull beginning to move over the sand. It went for only a couple of yards before the boat became stuck again.

'We're gonna kill the horses before we get it clear,' McCall complained, rubbing down the sweating neck of his spotted grey as Molina waded up. The other horse, a big-chested black, snorted and shook its head, blowing hard.

'They're helpin',' Molina said, patting the black's muzzle and almost being bitten for his trouble. 'Give 'em a rest, an' we'll try again.'

'Can you get your crew digging away some of the damn sand from under the boat? That'd help, surely.'

'It's a very dangerous job, workin' that low in shiftin' sand. They hit a pocket that collapses and they're under the boat as she rolls.'

McCall swore. 'Goddamnit, Molina! OK! Take the rest of that money I got from Wiley. It's not doing any good sitting in my saddle-bags. Give it to the crew – after your share, naturally – ' He said this sardonically and Molina acknowledged with a small nod. 'Get 'em digging. I've got to get down-river fast – If I miss that riverboat and Rosa, I'll come back for you, Molina. And not with any sack of gold.'

'Hey! Don't blame me! I'm tryin' to help!'

The prospect of a lengthy frustrating delay was getting to McCall now, after the long, long trail. To be this close to Kane – and Rosa – and be stuck in river mud. . . !

149

He forced himself to calm down. Getting agitated wouldn't help: he had to think clearly, allow Molina to run things: when a man had to rely upon people with expert knowledge of a situation it paid to take a back seat and let them get on with the job.

Even so, he allowed that if they hadn't made significant progress in two hours, he would saddle the grey and ride south, hoping to overtake the riverboat carrying Rosa – and Kane.

With something of a shock, he realized he was looking forward to squaring-off with Kane almost as much as he was looking forward to seeing Rosa again.

His trigger finger was definitely itchy.

Now Cooney was gone, the Mate was out of it, and Garrett was dead, there didn't seem to be anyone who could take charge.

If Garrett was still alive, probably the stranding would never have happened. Certainly he would have organized the attempts at refloating better. But Chief Engineer Gordie Struthers finally realized the predicament was far more important than his wonderful bird drawings, set them aside, reluctantly, and volunteered to look at the situation. He at least knew something about the river and how to overcome its obstacles, even if he did so from the depths of the gloomy engine room. Also, he'd been born on the Clyde. . . . On deck he walked around the canted decks, leaning far over the rail, making some notes in a small leather-covered book.

'Well, the fust thing we have to do is lighten the wee boatie. That means everyone not working to free the hull, goes ashore.'

He was the centre of attention, passengers crowding around, their weight unevenly distributed, and causing the big vessel to cant even more – not much, but every ounce would require an hour's work to regain equilibrium.

'You don't mean us, do you?' called the man in the tall beaverskin hat. 'We're paying passengers and we did not pay for this – this kind of inconvenience!'

'O' course ye didna', sur – but them's the way the cards've fallen, as they say – I'd be obleeged if ye'd take what luggage you can wi' you, too. Just stack it on the banks – we'll collect it again for you once we're afloat.'

There were angry protests from the passengers and Kane, having been drinking again, lurched out of his cabin and fired two shots into the air. Yorke came running, carrying a sawed-off shotgun, standing beside Kane.

The gunfire brought instant silence – and looks of apprehension. 'What the hell're you waitin' for? You heard the Irishman—'

'Scots, ye bletherin' heathen!' roared the engineer, face enpurpled.

'Yeah, OK. Can't unnerstand any of you, anyway.' Kane glanced at Yorke. 'Hurry 'em up – Give 'em one barrel.'

Yorke looked startled, at first thinking Kane meant shoot into the crowd, but realized quickly it was only meant to scare the griping passengers. He fired into the air, got over-enthusiastic and triggered the second barrel, too.

'Goddamnit!' hissed Kane, 'now I've gotta try an' hold 'em just with my Colt. . . ! Look at 'em! Ready to eat us alive. Reload, you stupid sonuver!'

The shotgun's thunder had brought Frenchy out of his cabin, still wearing his padre's robes – but clutching a huge Le Matt revolver. With his hair awry he looked like a madman. The crowd began to calm and when two more of Kane's men appeared, both carrying shotguns, they hurried to their cabins for their gear.

'See they move it along,' Kane snapped at his shot-gunners, two of the original Scattergun Gang, Woody and a hunchback with buck teeth called Marty.

They were both mean-eyed and pushed and hustled the complaining passengers. Twice they fired their shot-guns into the air, to hurry things along and within a half-hour the bedraggled and sorry-looking passengers were standing on the river bank amidst their scattered belongings.

'Watch out for snakes!' Kane called and laughed before swigging once more from his whiskey bottle.

Still grinning, he turned towards Frenchy and noticed the 'nuns' standing outside their cabin. 'Cookie' as he always thought of Rosa, was pale, worried looking.

But it was the other woman who claimed his atten-tion: she stood there, holding a cocked pistol in both hands as if she knew damn well how to use it.

McCall reined down, lifting an arm in annoyance as one of the branches of the trees he was riding through slapped back towards his face. He nudged the hard-

152

breathing grey out into a clearing, stood in the stirrups, listening. All he could hear were distant birds, the buzz of insects and rustling that likely meant snakes.

But he was sure he had heard distant shooting, too!

He started to curse the horse for breathing so hard, but patted its neck instead. He had ridden it hard since leaving the keelboat – still stranded way back there up the river. Progress had been made but it was too slow for him. Impatiently, he had unhitched the grey from the bows of the keelboat, saddled it while apologizing to the hard-worked mount, then swung into the saddle and rode off.

'Hey, McCall! – Come to Mooney's Landin' when you get back from Mexico! I'll buy you a drink!' called Molina.

'With *my* money!'

'Makes it taste better. 'Luck, *amigo*!'

He had ridden out without looking back then, driving the obedient grey harder than he liked. *Time was running out!* Originally, he had been content to catch up with the riverboat at Baton Rouge, even New Orleans. But he was too impatient now, had been dreaming about Rosa, *needed* to feel her in his arms, not just in some night-time fantasy. . . .

Molina had told him the banks were firm enough for several miles, but tended to be boggy and on the edge of quicksands not too far downstream. So far, he had been lucky and the grey had found firm footing. *They were shotguns he had heard!* he told himself emphatically. Damn right!

Distant, sure, but all he had to do was follow the

river. . . . He concentrated on riding. There were several snakes, rattlers, diamondbacks, and some water moccasins. He steered the frightened grey around them, not wanting to have to shoot and alert Kane or whoever it was ahead with the shotgun. The horse shied and rolled its eyes, giving him a baleful look.

He tweaked its ear and, though he was sure the horse didn't like him any better, they covered a lot of ground, crashing through brush, both man and animal receiving scratches.

The sun was way past the zenith. The trees seemed to close in on him. There was still a long way to go.

Then he reined-up, startled – incredulous. *A steamboat's whistle pierced the insect-laden afternoon, rapped his ears and senses – coming from around the next bend!*

Not only that, he could hear the threshing of the sternwheel as it churned the river to muddy froth in an effort to budge the hull from whatever was holding it fast!

He hastily checked Colt and rifle, urged the staggering grey on, slapping with the rein ends, reluctantly raking with the spurs. The animal snorted – *it would even the score some time!* But it crashed out of brush, McCall with rifle in hand, and he reined-up sharply.

There was a large crowd on the bank with luggage scattered over a wide area – passengers, he guessed, offloaded with some of the cargo to lighten the boat. They were all looking the other way, towards black smoke that roiled and belched from the tall stacks as the engine revved and the sternwheel thrashed and churned. The people began to cheer, some merely shouting encouragement.

McCall couldn't see that the boat was moving, but if they could hold the engines at that level of power, something had to give.

On board, everyone seemed to be on the river side, leaning over the rails, looking at the seething coffee-coloured water. Using *their* weight to help break the inshore suction he guessed. *As long as they kept looking down into the river and didn't turn and notice him. . . .*

Hoping there wasn't quicksand, he urged the weary grey into the water, edged out towards the bows, as everyone was concentrating on the stern now. The water wasn't very deep and he could have waded out but wanted the horse's height to make it easier to climb over the sides.

He almost made it undetected, and without reaching the quicksand that had claimed Cooney. But, standing on the saddle, balancing precariously as the grey tried to move on, McCall jumped for the side, hooked his free arm over the top and almost dropped the rifle. It clattered and one of the coloured crew at the rear of the crowd looking over the side, turned his head curiously. His eyes widened, white orbs against his dark skin, and his jaw dropped. Not taking his gaze off McCall as the man got a firmer footing, the mulatto shouted, over and over, '*Boss! Boss!*' and the crowd on deck spun quickly to see what all the excitement was about. . . .

In seconds, McCall recognized Marty the hunchback as the man brought up his scattergun. McCall didn't hesitate, triggered the rifle, skidded on the canted deck, and as he slid down to one knee, the shotgun thundered. It tore up the planks and some of the rico-cheting shot must have struck the crew and others who had been looking over the side. They yelled and scat-tered. McCall dropped flat as Woody opened fire, the charge of buckshot screaming overhead. He didn't know what was happening ashore as he rolled into the scuppers, worked the rifle's lever and trigger, getting off several shots.

Woody flung up his arms, hit the low rail and tumbled over into the churning river. Yorke brought his scattergun around and and braced the butt into his hip. McCall fired but knew it could only be a diversionary shot. He lunged out of the scuppers as a charge of buckshot sent splinters flying.

Yorke ran in, ready to fire the second barrel. McCall dropped his empty rifle and shoulder-rolled, going with the angle of the deck. It increased his speed and although he felt the sting of pellets in his back he knew he hadn't taken a bad wound. The sky and the belching smokestacks spun dizzily across his vision and then his Colt was banging and bucking against his wrist.

Yorke dropped to his knees, eyes wide, jaw loose, as bullets ripped into his chest. He started to fall but sud-denly Kane was there, grabbing the dying man's shirt, hauling him upright as a shield. He fired under Yorke's arm and McCall felt the searing burn of lead across his left cheek. His ear stung, too, and he felt warm blood running down his neck. Kane bared his teeth, jerked the now dead Yorke in front of him again and brought up his smoking Colt.

McCall, momentraily dazed by his wounds, stretched out on the deck, realizing he now made a better target. He spun on to his side, sixgun coming around as Kane laughed, and dropped Yorke's body. Then something blurred behind Kane's head and he jerked, half-turning. McCall glimpsed a nun – *a nun!* – standing over the dazed Kane, holding a short iron bar in both hands. As he stared, she ripped off the headpiece, both hands bound apparently, and the beautiful golden hair spilled around the pale face, the golden vision which had kept him going these long weeks. . . .

'Rosa!' he breathed.

Then Kane spun and clawed at her but she dropped the iron bar on the man's foot and he lurched away from her. Crouching, Kane looked up at McCall, Rosa clambering away from behind him.

'You won't shoot!' he taunted McCall. 'I've lost my gun – I'm unarmed . . . you could never live with killin' an unarmed man in cold blood, not you, McCall!'

'Don't bet on it, Kane!' McCall said and fired.

Kane went down, clutching his right shoulder, making strangling sounds as he tried not to scream with the agony of a shattered collar bone.

He bared his teeth. 'B-bastard! But you – won't take me – in. . . .'

With a mighty effort he heaved up, thrust Rosa aside so she fell on the deck as he leaped over the rail.

Almost instantly there was a scream that froze the blood of McCall and everyone else on the deck. He looked overside – Kane had landed on the splintered, shattered stump of one of the old trees the *Centurion* had crashed into when she ran aground. Impaled, he twitched feebly, arms swinging weakly, coughing blood, and was finally still.

'Josh, watch out!'

McCall spun at the warning from Rosa, saw a priest – *a priest now!* – running at him with a massive revolver held in both hands. He fired and the gun jerked his arms up almost over his head. McCall heard the air-whip of the large slug passing overhead. The smoking muzzle followed him as he dropped to the deck and rolled – uphill this time. It was a muscle-wrenching effort but the Frenchman had fired into the scuppers, figuring McCall had to go with the cant of the deck. By the time he lifted the heavy gun and spun round, McCall, on his back, fired once. The Frenchman's head jerked violently and his long body hit the rail and toppled over into the river.

McCall twisted awkwardly as he heard a woman grunt or make some sort of hurting noise, and was in time to see another nun – *another one!* – topple into the scup-pers, blood oozing from a deep gash across her forehead beneath the nun headpiece. She fell untidily and McCall got slowly to his feet as Rosa stumbled up, holding her short iron, now gleaming with Carmella's blood.

McCall dropped his gun back into the holster after making sure no one else was ready to take a shot at him and ripped at the cords binding Rosa's wrists. The cords hadn't even fallen from her hands when she threw her arms about McCall's neck and the sobbing sound she made was from his own arms tightening convulsively about her slim, clinging body, squeezing the air from her lungs in his enthusiasm.

'I dreamt about you last night,' he said thickly. 'Just had to come looking for the real thing.'

She smiled, emotion keeping her from speaking right then. She touched his bloody cheek, kissed it lightly.

'The scar can only improve my looks,' McCall joked and gestured to the unconscious woman in the scuppers. 'Who the hell is she?'

'The Frenchman's sister, he was trying to get her away into Mexico.'

McCall looked puzzled. 'Why? What'd she done. . . ?'

Rosa smiled faintly and knelt beside the unconscious Carmella, throwing back the nun's habit, revealing the bandage patch on her upper left arm.

'She been shot?'

Rosa smiled and began to take off the bandage. 'She wanted everyone to think so, but she was wearing it for another reason – we shared quarters, you know, and – see?'

Under the bandage was a small tattoo. 'Looks like a spider,' McCall said and instantly knew what he was seeing. 'God almighty! *She's* – The Spider? The assassin. . . ?'

'She told me she likes to be known as The Black Widow. Yes, she was on the run when she failed to kill the president and this was Frenchy's way of getting her out of the country. *He* was in trouble, too. His last duel was with someone from a very powerful family and he would have been hanged if he was caught – so they were both very eager to get to Mexico . . . killing must run in the family. That mission, Los Pobre, had caused him some kind of hurt years ago – he saw his chance to get his revenge – and also to get the nuns' habits and the Holy Father's robes as disguise.'

'And you had to go along with these maniacs just so Kane could sell you for a high price.'

'It doesn't matter now, Josh.' She clung to his arm, rubbed her head against his shoulder, her lovely hair touching his face. 'Nothing matters now. We're back together.'

He tightened his arms about her. 'Yeah, that's all that matters.'